Chasing Rainbows

Other books by Julia Clarke

Chasing Rainbows

Julia Clarke

OXFORD
UNIVERSITY PRESS

OXFORD
UNIVERSITY PRESS

Great Clarendon Street, Oxford OX2 6DP

Oxford University Press is a department of the University of Oxford.
It furthers the University's objective of excellence in research, scholarship,
and education by publishing worldwide in

Oxford New York

Auckland Bangkok Buenos Aires
Cape Town Chennai Dar es Salaam Delhi Hong Kong Istanbul
Karachi Kolkata Kuala Lumpur Madrid Melbourne Mexico City Mumbai
Nairobi São Paulo Shanghai Taipei Tokyo Toronto

Oxford is a registered trade mark of Oxford University Press
in the UK and in certain other countries

British Library Cataloguing in Publication Data available

ISBN 0 19 275326 6

1 3 5 7 9 10 8 6 4 2

Printed in Great Britain

For all the dancers in my family—especially Pauline,
my mother, Sonia, Janis,
Josephine, and Bethany

Acknowledgement:
Mermaid by Michael Clarke.
Clockwork Heart by Karl Culley.

1

It is while I am sitting in Ash's kitchen that the idea comes to me. An arranged marriage could be a very good thing. For a parent, that is . . .

It is Jessica Browne's party that starts it all off. It is the first really interesting party that I have ever been invited to. It has all the right ingredients.

1) Boys—Jessica's brother, Joshua, is 17 and the talk of the school because he's so wild and good-looking. I have had a secret crush on him all this term.

2) Drinks—Jessica says Josh makes a mean punch with mysterious and exotic ingredients. But then everything about Joshua Browne is mysterious and exotic!

3) Absent parents—it is Jessica's mother and stepfather's first wedding anniversary; they are having a romantic weekend away. I am under strict instructions to bring a friend—namely Ash—a sleeping bag, and a packet of Resolve for the inevitable hangover . . . Wow!

While Ash makes us cappuccinos I muse on the wonder of this invitation. I feel like Cinderella on her way to the ball. It is totally wonderful to be asked—if a bit scary. Jessica is really fussy about who she allows into her posse. They are usually all the really cool people with designer clothes and attitude. It is still a puzzle to me why she has invited me. But I am busy inventing a whole scenario about her bro—the utterly mesmerizing Joshua. Something along the lines of him saying that he's seen me around—or better still in the school production of *Grease* when I played Sandy—and would she please ask me along to the party. Not at all likely, but it can't hurt to pretend—can it?

'Rosie! Are you OK? I've asked you three times if you want chocolate sprinkles and all you've given me is a zombie stare! You also appear to be talking to yourself.' Ash is leaning against the worktop staring hard at me; there is the merest hint of a frown on his freckled face. 'I suppose it's impossible to expect conversation from a party chick. You'll soon be too cool to share oxygen with the rest of us.' I wait for a laugh from him, but it doesn't come. Ash is the most laid-back person I've ever met and this comment is just about the nearest he gets to irritable.

'No sprinkles, thanks. And please don't offer me a cookie,' I add earnestly. 'I'm dieting and praying I can get into my embroidered jeans by Saturday. I've grown so much since last year they hardly fit me.'

'Don't be stupid,' Ash scoffs. 'You're far too skinny to diet and anyway you can't lose weight in a week.' He puts a whole cookie into his mouth and pulls silly faces at me as he eats it.

'You can if you don't eat anything at all. I lost loads when I had gastric flu.'

'You're bonkers, Rose. You were so weak then you couldn't get out of bed for days. You even had to have a potty chair in the bedroom. Fat lot of use having to be carried into Jessica Browne's wonderful party on a stretcher . . .' He ducks his head away from me and looks down into his mug of coffee while I stare at him, hurt, my lower lip pouting.

'Thanks for reminding me about the potty chair, very gallant of you . . .' I mutter.

There is a long uneasy silence in the kitchen, just the tick-tock of the replica ship's clock on the wall. We don't have any old-fashioned clocks in our house because my mother says she can't bear to hear time slipping away by the second, so the clock in Ash's kitchen always sounds extra loud to me.

2

Ash switches on the radio to hide the prolonged pause in our conversation. It's then that the full implication of Jessica's party starts to bite. I have a problem. My best friends are Ash and Ellen and we usually do everything together. Ash is even good at doing girl things like clothes shopping and buying Christmas presents. Because he's the tallest and the cleverest lad in our year no one ever gives him any stick about hanging out with me and Ellen. I think he could take up knitting and make it fashionable among the boys. But this party is different because I want them both to come with me. Jessica seems to have made up her mind that Ash will join me—'Bring Ash with you,' she commanded. That's fine—but I hate to leave Ellen out.

The other problem is my mother. It's not that she won't let me go—I've been away to Guide camp and on holiday to Devon with Ellen and her family. It's just that over the last year I've had these niggling worries.

'Do you worry about your father when you go out?' I ask Ash.

'What?' he says, giving me a blank look.

'Your father, do you worry about him?'

'I thought we were talking about dieting,' he mutters, biting into another biscuit. I reach for a cookie and begin to nibble at it. He grins at me.

I realize that I will have to elaborate if I want a proper answer from him and suddenly I feel disloyal to my mother. Also I can't quite pin down what I am feeling and why.

For a while I am silent, but then I say in a rush: 'It's just that when you're little, you know how it is, you do everything with them, especially at weekends. And it's all a big deal: you know, Hallowe'en and bonfire night and Christmas and Easter eggs—and going away during the holidays. And now they still want to be doing all that kid's stuff and go shopping with you. And, when you go out in the evening, they have nothing to do but sit around and worry about what time you'll be home . . .' My voice trails off. I sound horribly mean and totally selfish. I can't continue. Anyway, maybe it's different for Ash and his dad.

'My father's on duty most of the time at evenings and weekends,' Ash says a bit apologetically. What he really means is that either he hasn't noticed, or is too kind to admit, that my mother needs to get herself a social life.

'It's just that she works all the time if she doesn't do things with me,' I mutter.

Ash shrugs. 'My dad goes to the gym or out running when he's not working.'

I brighten. Maybe what Mum needs is a hobby.

At that moment Ash's father's car draws into the courtyard that separates our homes. I crunch my biscuit up and gulp at my coffee. Mum told me when Ash and his dad, Ralph, moved in that we mustn't get too friendly or it could be claustrophobic. She doesn't know that Ash and I have fallen into the habit of chillin' in his kitchen after school. I always try to avoid Ralph just in case he ever drops it into conversation with my mother that the coach house is now like my second home.

'You don't have to rush,' Ash says kindly. 'You know he always goes shopping after the ante-natal clinic; they can't have been very busy, and that's why he's back early.'

Ralph edges his estate car up to the door and begins to unload boxes of groceries. He is unbelievably well-organized and doesn't agree with using plastic bags. He could bore for England telling you about landfill sites and how long plastic takes to disintegrate. He has all these nifty stacking boxes which he keeps in the boot of his car. He has different colours for different types of things so it's easy to put the shopping away when he gets home.

He and Ash begin to stash all the stuff he's bought. Because the coach house is so small it's been fitted out like a ship's cabin with turntable cupboards and a table that folds away—a little origami room. 'Let me help,' I say, and I take the cool box. Ash opens the freezer for me. It's disguised as a cupboard which is neat. The whole kitchen is like the inside of a clock, everything fits with precision. I look down at the drawers of the freezer. They are beautifully arranged, all the bread in one drawer, meat in another, veg in the next. I begin to unpack the box making sure I don't mess up the system.

'Well done, Rose, thanks very much,' Ralph says. He is washing his hands briskly at the sink. I think to myself, not for the first time, that it's just as well that me and Mum didn't move into the coach house, which Mum suggested at one point, because you have to be a really well-organized sort of person to live in such a confined space.

'Supper in forty-five minutes,' Ralph says. He puts on a crisply-ironed blue and white striped butcher's apron. Then he gets out all the ingredients and utensils for their meal; laying out the chopping board and razor-sharp knives in a row as if he's going to operate on the chicken. I suppose it's impossible to ever really switch off if you're a doctor. 'Then we'll swim later if you haven't got too much homework, Ashley. If not I'll go on my own. Would you like to come with us, Rose?' he adds kindly. 'It's marvellous exercise, you know, and a good stress reliever.'

'Oh, that's kind of you, but I've got a project to work on,' I lie. I made the mistake of going swimming with them once and I'll never do it again. On the rare occasions Mum and I swim we mess about, playing games and duck diving. But Ash and his dad are serious swimmers. It's up and down the pool like robots. They even count how many lengths they've done! It's fanatical and totally not fun. I was exhausted afterwards and had to eat two bars of Galaxy before I felt better.

I watch Ralph's brown efficient hands chopping onions, and think that if I ever need an operation I'd like him to do it for me. Then suddenly the thought comes to me that he and Mum really couldn't be more different— and it's at that moment a gigantic light bulb goes on in my head, like it does in cartoons. I realize that together they would be perfect. Mum would brighten him up a bit and he would organize her. It would be a marriage made in heaven.

An arranged marriage—arranged by me! With maybe a little bit of help from Ash. What could be more perfect?

I am so knocked out by this thought that I badly need to be alone to let it sink in. I am almost afraid that I might blurt out the ideas that are roaring around in my head. It would be truly dreadful if I suddenly yelled: 'Hey! I've had a brilliant idea. Ralph, how about getting it together with my ma? You're a sad widower and she's a single mum who hasn't had a boyfriend since the year dot—or to be more precise the year before I was born. You would be good together—a perfect couple.'

I think of my mother: her long pale pre-Raphaelite curls, which cascade down over her shoulders because she never has time for the hairdresser, and her tall willowy frame and gentle blue eyes. Physically she is the exact opposite of Ralph's square face, broad shoulders, and dark hair. And they say opposites attract—don't they? They'd look lovely together—like something off a book cover!

I nip at my lip with my front teeth to keep any impetuous words in check. But it is difficult. It is such an unbelievably wonderful brainwave that I am desperate to share it with someone. But I get a grip and mumble something about going home to do my ballet warm-up, and then I scuttle towards the door, avoiding looking at them both.

'Are you all right, Rose?' Ralph asks, concerned. His doctor's intuition has picked up on my mood.

'Fine, fine.' I give him a brilliant smile. 'See you later, Ash,' I add. And as I cross the courtyard I have to stop myself from leaping into the air because it could look seriously bonkers. But I am just so excited. And I don't understand why I haven't thought about this before. It could be the answer to all our problems.

Our big kitchen seems cool after the cosy warmth of the coach house. Ralph and Ash have the sun streaming in through their window all day, but we don't get any sun at all on this side of the house so our kitchen is always cold, reaching arctic proportions in the winter. This room is the only one that looks directly across the courtyard to the coach house, so when it was sold Mum nailed a makeshift calico blind over our window for privacy. That was three years ago. The calico is now thick and cobwebby and laced with the corpses of many insects, so the light in the kitchen is eerie and greenish, like being under water.

I light the gas oven; it is old, like everything in the house, and takes ages to get hot. Then I wander upstairs, thinking about my wonderful plan. Ralph has never seen our house properly. Mum invited him over for a sherry on the evening they moved in. He and Ash came to the front door, which I thought weird as our back door faces their door, but anyway that's what they did. And Mum ushered them into the front sitting room and it was all very stiff and starchy, with Ralph making polite conversation about the garden.

For ages after they came to live in the coach house Ralph used to offer to have a go at our part of the garden, coming up with suggestions on how he could hack back the bushes and cut down trees to let in more light. But Mum said 'No thank you' so often he eventually stopped offering. I have never worked out whether Mum really likes gardening or not. I don't think so. So she should have jumped at the chance of having someone 'tidy it up' as Ralph so kindly put it. I hate having to cut the grass. Sometimes, when Mum spends a day out in the garden, she reminds me of a goddess of destruction or some mad woman from the Greek myths: hair wild with twigs and leaves, hands bloodied with sap juice from mutilated bushes, and outside a patch of wilderness savagely flattened. But unfortunately it's not like Ralph's gardening. When he does things they stay done. With Mum nothing she does ever really makes much difference. Maybe she's not hard enough on the plants—because within a couple of days the savaged patch goes back to looking exactly as it did before.

Our garden looks even more derelict next to the little patch that belongs to the coach house. Ralph keeps it immaculate, with lovely bright flowers standing in line, like so many marigold soldiers, and it definitely makes our jungle look worse. I smile at the thought of Ralph making the whole of the garden look like a flower show. The more I think about this arranged marriage the more attractive it seems.

Apart from the kitchen the only other window in our house which overlooks the coach house kitchen is the small stained-glass skylight on the stairs. Mum didn't bother to cover this as it's difficult to see through— difficult, but not impossible. There is a tiny pane of pink glass that has faded over the years to the colour of washed-out petals. If I sit on the stairs and lean forward, I can glimpse through and get a rose-tinted glance at Ash and Ralph's kitchen. Ash is washing up. Ralph is drying. Such efficiency! I give another sigh of contentment.

After I have dropped my bag in my bedroom I go downstairs and start thrashing around in the freezer. I have an amazing plan. I will get supper ready. And then, while we are eating, I will talk to Mum about staying over at Jessica's.

2

Mum is late. She puts her briefcase down in the hallway next to the umbrella stand; it is jumbled with ancient hockey sticks, walking canes, and brollies that belonged to bygone relatives. She brings a pile of books into the kitchen and places them carefully on the table. 'Are you all right?' she asks anxiously. 'I left a message. Why didn't you pick the phone up?'

The wrong answer would be that I'd slipped over to Ash's to watch a video while Ralph went for his swim. The right answer is to mumble something about homework which is basically truthful but fudges the issue of whether I have actually done it or not.

Ash and I did discuss it: 'Ash, have you done your maths?'

'No—you?'

'No. Can I call you later?'

'Course.'

'Thanks—you're a pal.'

Ash is brilliant at just about everything. When he explains maths, even I understand. The school should pay him because he's the only thing which got me and Ellen through our SATS.

'I've put a casserole from the freezer in the oven for supper,' I say brightly.

'Thank you, darling. I'm sorry I'm late. End of term papers to mark. And then the new poetry professor arrived unexpectedly—we went out for some tea. He's read my book, which is quite something, isn't it?'

She is still looking anxious. I give her a hug. 'Sorry about the phone. I'll try to catch it next time. I was fine, really. Did this new professor say he liked your work?'

My mother looks away, shy as a child: 'Well—yes he did. He was very . . .' she pauses, suddenly lost in thought. 'He was very complimentary.'

'Which poem did he like the best?' I question.

'Well, he didn't say. But from the way he was talking I think it might have been your favourite—"Mermaid".'

'Ah, a man of good taste,' I tease. 'All the poems in your book are brilliant, but "Mermaid" is mega brilliant, no wonder he liked it.'

Mum's cheeks are quite pink and she is smiling. A little flame of optimism lights up inside me. She'll let me stay over at Jessica's—no problem.

'There's something I want to talk to you about, over supper,' she adds, her face suddenly darkening.

'OK,' I say carefully. I don't add that there is something I want to talk to her about too. I am not going to rush into this request for an all-night ticket. Ash always says I approach everything in life like an out-of-control Chieftain tank. Tonight I am going to be subtle and not blow it.

To prove how mature and responsible I am I cook some potatoes in the pressure cooker and get some frozen peas ready simmering in a pan while Mum sorts out her books. 'Now, leave it all to me,' I say when she tries to help. I set the table carefully, hunting for two plates without cracks and folding the kitchen roll we use for napkins into water-lily shapes. And when everything is ready and Mum is sitting at the table, I happily bring the casserole out of the oven, hoping for a fragrant whiff of savoury meat and veg—but there is nothing. I carefully put the dish down on the table, remove the tin-foil cover and find to my horror that I am looking down at a charred-looking crumble with acid-green juice bubbling at the edges. This is not the rip-roaring success I was hoping for and I pray quickly to the god of small ambitions it is not an omen.

Then, to make matters worse, my eyes fill with tears. I think it's partly stress because I am working myself up to asking my mother about Jessica's party, but it's also disappointment because I am really hungry. Goodness knows how I ever thought I could stop eating for a week! The thought of missing one meal, or the prospect of dining on just boiled potatoes and peas, pushes me right over the edge.

'Oh, I'm sorry, sweetheart, it's all my fault. I didn't label it—did I?' Mum says, hugging me and wiping the tears from my face with her hand. 'Don't cry. How about if I walk down to the main road to get us some fish and chips? If I jog back they'll still be hot. And if you put that crumble back in the oven we could have it with some custard. Though, now I come to think about it, I'm not really sure how old it is. We didn't have any gooseberries in the garden last year, did we? They were all mildewy. Maybe it would be best to chuck it.'

We both stare down at the crumble. It does look septic. 'Pop the plates into the oven to warm. I'll only be about ten minutes,' Mum says, kissing my cheek. 'Save the potatoes, we'll have them cold tomorrow,' she adds as she goes out. A minute later she pops her head around the door. 'I can't find my purse. I'm a hopeless mother, aren't I? Pass me five pounds, will you please, poppet.'

I reach up to the ornamental teapot on the shelf above the cooker where we keep our emergency fund of housekeeping money and pass her a note. 'I won't be long,' she adds. 'Cheer up.'

'I'm fine; I'll butter some bread. And you're not hopeless—you're great,' I add, but she is already gone and I hear the front door close.

I put the potatoes in the pantry and fill the kettle so we can have mugs of tea with our meal and pretend we are at Harry Ramsden's. I am just scraping the crumble into the bin and cursing it for looking and smelling so foul, when the doorbell chimes. I assume it's Mum and she's left her key; and I scamper, desperate as a puppy for its supper, to the front door and fling it open. To my horror and disappointment it isn't Mum with fish and chips but a strange man, standing on our doorstep holding my mother's handbag.

It's way too late to do what I am meant to do—which is to use the security chain and check who it is before I open the door—so I decide to brazen it out. 'Hi—can I help you?' I say loudly.

'Hey now, lassie—' The rest of the words are unintelligible. I've never heard anyone with such a strong Scottish accent. But I get the gist of what he is saying. I am being told off for not using the chain and opening the door to him. Honestly, the cheek of some people! But in a way it is reassuring because I am sure axe murderers don't harangue their victims for opening the door to them before they hack them up. I decide to ignore his lecture. Instead I hold out my hand for the bag.

'I take it you are returning my mother's handbag. How very kind,' I say regally. 'Maybe you should leave your name and phone number as I'm sure my mother will want to thank you properly herself.'

'Where is she now then, ma bonny girl?'

Now 'lassie' is bad enough but to be addressed as 'ma bonny girl' is altogether too much. The man laughs as if he can read my mind.

'I'm Hamish MacCrimmon, her new colleague at work. She told me about you. We had some tea together and your mother left her bag.' He articulates all this very slowly and carefully—as if I am foreign or a sandwich short of a picnic.

I am tempted to say she is in the bath, but finding out that I am talking to the new poetry professor from the university gives me such a jolt that I blurt out the truth: 'She's run down to the main road, to the chip shop, for some supper.'

'Walking?'

'Yes, of course, we don't have a car.'

He holds out my mother's bag and says something about going down to fetch her as it's a fair stretch but he's lapsed into dialect again and I get only an approximation of what he is saying. His eyes crinkle and he laughs again, just as if I have said out loud what I am thinking. My mother has always told me I have an expressive face but this is getting scary.

I take her bag from him and watch him walk away. To my mind that man didn't look how a professor of poetry should look. Dr Granger, the last one, had wild white hair that stood in a halo around his head and he wore a grey suit so faded and threadbare it looked as if he had been born in it. That man looked like a workman, with sinewy arms and an ugly weathered face. Also, he was really clean and smart in a T-shirt that screamed 'I've just been ironed', crisp jeans, and highly polished shoes. No one else at the university looks like that—ironed T-shirts and shiny shoes might just be considered seriously weird.

I slam the door, annoyed with myself. I have really messed up. If he tells my mother I opened the door to him she will flip—she's really hyper about things like that. Also, the failure of supper just reinforces the idea that I am a silly little kid instead of nearly grown-up and able to cope. Just for a moment I want to go and peep through the rose-tinted glass and glimpse Ash and Ralph's perfect kitchen but suddenly it seems a really childish thing to be doing, spying on them like that. I swallow hard. It seems light years since I had lunch and I had only one cookie after school. I blink back tears and make myself a cup of tea, and then I eat one of the pieces of bread and butter. I must be cool, calm, and collected when my mother gets back, if I am to have any chance of going to Jessica's on Saturday.

My mother doesn't come back for absolutely ages; I eat all the bread and butter and drink all the tea in the pot. I am so desperate I even start to regret throwing away the crumble, thinking that it might have been all right smothered in hot creamy custard or disguised with a huge dollop of vanilla ice-cream.

Eventually my mother returns. Hamish MacCrimmon is with her carrying a big cardboard box full of food. They have been to Sainsbury's, and he must have paid because there're all sorts in there—far more than five pounds would ever buy.

Mum's face is flushed and she is nervous. She says something about money and hovers by the teapot on the shelf above the cooker but Hamish MacCrimmon brushes it off. They unpack the food—gorgeous smoked salmon, packets of lettuce, and dinky little containers full of coleslaw and potato salad, just the kind of convenience food we never have because it is too expensive. I turn my back on them and pour the wasted peas down the sink. They are now the colour and consistency of sludge. I squish them through the plughole viciously. Everything has gone wrong, and now this man is staying for supper. The question of the party is racing around in my mind like a hamster on a wheel. I feel as if I will scream if I don't get a chance to ask Mum about it.

We sit around the table. I eat solidly, ploughing through everything. My mother and Mr MacCrimmon talk; not about poetry, now that would be interesting, I like listening to stuff like that. No. They talk about the roof, the chimney pots, and the guttering of our house. Fascinating! Why does a poetry professor want to yak on about flashing and slates and down-pipes? It's bizarre. It's just as well the food is good. There's even a fresh-cream sponge for pudding. Heaven!

Then, just as I am starting on my second bit of cake, and hoping Mr MacCrimmon will disappear very soon, Mum starts telling him all kinds of personal and private things. She seems to have forgotten about her piece of cake; instead she leans on the table, her chin in her hand, her lovely hair flowing to one side. Her eyes are tragic, and Hamish MacCrimmon stares at her sympathetically in a way I find annoying, while she tells him about her auntie May leaving us the house.

'Rose and I lived here with my aunt May while I was at university. I would never have managed as a single mother studying for a degree and then an MA without her help,' Mum says. And her blue eyes fill, as they always do when she talks about Auntie May dying. 'She left me the house in her Will because she was worried Rose and I would be homeless.'

'God bless her,' Hamish MacCrimmon says, his Scottish voice soft as a prayer. Mum manages a tiny watery smile.

'She left my brother, Milo, what money she had. The house is worth far more; or it would be if it wasn't falling down. That's why I sold the coach house, to even things out a bit for him.'

Mum blushes, as she always does when she has to talk about Milo, my wicked good-for-nothing uncle. He's a failed rock star. Sometimes, in discount shops, and especially at car boot sales, you still see copies of his LPs. There he is on the front covers, waist-length hair held in place by a bandana, war-paint on his face, freaking out with his guitar. Ash's uncle is a bank manager who sends him big cheques at Christmas and birthday: some people have all the luck. Because Milo only ever gets in touch with Mum to ask for a 'loan' and I don't think he's ever bought me a present in the whole of my life.

Mum is telling Hamish MacCrimmon everything about the house; not just the problems with the roof, but all about the boiler and how the heating doesn't work and everything else that's wrong with it—it's awful! Honestly, you'd think we lived in a slum to hear her . . .

'I know it would really be more sensible to sell it,' she says. 'I do know that. But it belonged to Aunt May's grandfather and so it's been in the family for generations.

It seems wrong somehow to let it go just because I am so feeble. And, of course, Rose has lived here all her life and we do love it, don't we?' she says, smiling at me. I nod, trying not to scowl. Normally, we never talk about these things, apart from to each other.

Then she does the most extraordinary thing. She offers to show him round the house. I am so surprised that I choke on my last piece of sponge cake and cough so much that a big blob of cream shoots from my mouth onto my plate. I am really embarrassed and double-furious now. I don't like having shocks when I am eating. This simply isn't fair. We don't take people upstairs—ever!

But when I have finished eating, and the left-over food has been put in the fridge, and Hamish MacCrimmon has insisted on doing the washing up, she takes him on a tour of the house. I don't go with them; I am too dismayed by what is happening. I go into the sitting room, turn on the TV, throw myself into one of the big old leather armchairs and flick through the channels. There is nothing to watch and my mood is grim. I wish suddenly, fervently, that we weren't poor: and that we had Sky and a DVD player, or even a TV that wasn't like watching the programme through a snowstorm.

Hamish MacCrimmon puts his head round the door to say goodbye to me. I hardly bother to reply. Then, when Mum comes into the sitting room, I can't stop myself and I blurt out: 'I've been invited to Jessica's house on Saturday, can I stay over?'

'Is it a sleepover?' Mum asks brightly, like an echo from the days when I wore My Little Pony pyjamas.

'It's a party,' I mutter.

'How lovely. Is it Jessica's birthday?'

'No.'

'So what's the party for?' Mum asks. This is terrible— next thing she'll be asking if there's going to be a conjurer and party bags.

'Nothing really—her brother has finished his exams and it's nearly end of term.'

'Oh . . .' Mum looks a bit baffled.

'Ash and Ellen are going,' I say. I was going to say Ash was going but suddenly I realize I can't go without Ellen and I'll have to ask Jessica if I can take both of them. Surely one more won't make much difference at a rave? Anyway, Mum might feel it's OK if both of them are there.

'Oh . . .' Now Mum looks baffled and worried. 'Jessica's parents will be there, won't they?' she asks.

'Yes, I should think so; they live there, don't they?' I mutter miserably.

'I'll speak to Ellen's mother and see what we can sort out. Where does Jessica live?'

'Thornley,' I say quietly.

'That's miles away,' Mum says shocked.

'Not if you've got a car it isn't,' I say with a sigh. This isn't going the way I planned at all. I can see my chances of dancing the night away receding by the minute.

'I need to talk to you about something really important,' Mum says.

'OK,' I say sulkily. Jessica's party is really important to me, but she doesn't seem to have sussed that out.

'Milo phoned me today,' Mum says.

'Well, I hope he didn't want money, because we haven't got any,' I say with a sniff.

'He's been offered the chance of a recording contract with a band in America and he's desperate to go. I was shocked to learn that Jasmine left several months ago to work on cruise ships and he's been bringing the two little girls up on his own. He needs someone to look after them while he's away. He says he'll be earning good money and he'll pay for their keep.'

'What?' I say, shocked.

'He wants us to have them over the summer, from next week when school finishes. I said I'd have to think about it.'

Mum chews at her fingernail, looking worried. I am dumb-struck for a moment. And it's not often that happens to me. I've never met my cousins—or Jasmine their mother—though I know she is a professional dancer.

'It's not the money so much,' Mum says anxiously. 'I've the chance of some extra work over the summer for Professor MacCrimmon. So we could probably just about manage financially. It's the responsibility. Crystal is nearly twelve and Cara just four.' Mum shivers suddenly. 'I never let you out of my sight when you were that age. They'll need an awful lot of looking after. And you've got your rehearsals and dance show to think about. I don't know that we've got the time to care for them.'

'Crystal dances, doesn't she?' I say, thinking back to the only photograph we were ever sent of Crystal when she was little. No one has bothered to send us a photo of Cara so I have no idea at all what she looks like. 'Do you remember?' I ask Mum. 'They sent us a lovely picture of her in a tutu—she was the babiest cygnet in a show and she was really sweet.'

I warm suddenly to these cousins I have never met. And then I think about Mum and how attractive she will be to Ralph with two dear little girls in tow. Ralph is really keen on doing your bit for society. He's always banging on about social responsibility. Mum will be far more interesting to him looking after other people's children than writing lots of poems that he doesn't understand. English is the one subject where I outshine Ash—he and Ralph think reading a book is studying the Volvo manual for their car. My mother's poetry is a complete mystery to them.

'Let's do it, Mum,' I say suddenly. 'The show isn't a problem. I could take them along to Mrs Valente and ask if she could give them a part.' My brain is racing with ideas and organization and I'm getting quite excited. 'We'd have to pay for their costumes; but Mrs Valente is giving me free costumes and even paying me a bit for helping with all the babies and chaperoning during rehearsals, so I don't need costume money or much pocket money. I'm going to be too busy to go shopping,' I add. And I make a tiny prayer that I don't grow too much these holidays and my embroidered jeans last a while longer.

'Oh, Rose, that's so kind and generous of you,' Mum cries, giving me a hug. 'You shame me, you really do. I was only thinking of how much work and worry they would be. Are you sure you don't mind looking after them during rehearsals?'

'Of course not,' I say. 'No problem.'

I've been going to the Valente Academy since I was three. I am the most senior of the seniors and Mrs Valente's right-hand helper. I get serious respect and worship from all the little ones, who treat me like a god.

'They couldn't come to any harm at the rehearsals, now could they?' Mum says. 'And it would be lovely for them. I don't think they've had much of a life in the last few months. Jasmine and Milo have moved around so much it must have been very unsettling for them. And I don't know how Milo will have coped on his own. Even when he and Jasmine were together they always seemed to be short of cash.'

I think back to the sunny face of the small girl in the photograph. 'It'll be all right,' I say easily. In my mind I imagine lazy summer picnics on the lawn with the four of us and Ash and Ralph. It is sure to result in Ralph viewing my mother in a whole new light—seeing not just a rather disorganized poet but a lovely, selfless Lady Bountiful. I will make sure he knows how self-sacrificing and noble my mother has been and it is bound to make a difference. At least one part of my life is going to plan. Because I've got a nasty feeling I'm going to have uphill work with Mum about Jessica's party.

3

Jessica is plainly furious with me, although she tries quite hard to hide it. I feel a bit confused. I don't really see why it matters to her if I stay over or not. She must have heaps of really interesting people going to her party. Why should she care about me? I try to feel flattered. Maybe she has heard I was a riot at Guide camp? And that I'm likely to organize *Fame Academy* auditions and midnight feasts with cider and chocolate . . .

Jessica pouts, raking perfect silvery nails through long straight blonde hair (the girl has everything). While I stand in front of her like some stupid little kid being interrogated by a teacher, acutely aware of my frizzy hair and bitten fingernails.

'I'm sorry, Jessica,' I say, looking down at the ground, feeling humiliated. No. Worse than that—not just humble and gawky, but also awash with some deeper, indefinable gut emotion that I can't fathom. Why is she making me feel like this . . . just because I can't sleep over at her stupid old party? I'm starting to think I shan't bother going after all. My jeans don't fit even though I've been doing double warm-ups and stomach crunches and haven't touched a piece of chocolate for days.

'Ellen gets awful headaches if she doesn't get enough sleep,' I say apologetically. 'And, as her parents are going out to dinner, they have said they will come over to fetch us. It won't be until half eleven or nearly midnight.'

'Well that's OK for Ellen—but what about you and

Ashley? You don't get headaches, do you?' Jessica is positively sulky.

I think back to when Ash asked Ralph about the party. He was completely relaxed about it. 'Fine, stay over if you want,' he said. 'But if you are coming back late don't make any noise, will you, because I'm on duty next day.'

Why is everything so much easier for boys? In complete contrast to Ralph, my mother has been fussing like a hen with a newly-hatched chick. You'd think I was asking to do something really exciting and dangerous. At this rate I'll never be able to do anything truly interesting, like walking to the North Pole or sailing around the world, because my mother will be too busy panicking about whether I am getting enough sleep and eating properly.

'Ash and I will be going home with Ellen,' I say a bit mulishly. I am getting fed up with this inquisition.

'Please yourself, but you'll be missing out on all the fun,' Jessica says, shrugging a slim shoulder. She always wears a tiny gold choker under her shirt: it is fragile and glittery like fairy gold and even though the school has a strict no-jewellery rule she gets away with it. That's the kind of girl Jessica is—she always gets her own way. But not this time. Thanks to Ellen's mother and mine getting together like a pair of old fishwives and organizing our lives down to the last detail. Ridiculously I feel resentful towards everyone—even Ash—because he could stay over if he wanted to, but has volunteered to come back with me and Ellen.

I have a go at him after school; and, as I am drinking some wonderful hot chocolate he has made for me, I feel bad about it but I can't stop myself. I scoop some of the grated chocolate off the froth with my finger and lick it carefully. I have serious withdrawal symptoms from giving up sweets and biscuits. Maybe this is why I am becoming so bad-tempered? If I had a KitKat I'd probably feel like a completely different person.

'Jessica's dead miffed that we're all leaving early on

Saturday. Why don't you stay over? She says we'll be missing out on all the fun.'

'Why? What will they be doing?' Ash asks with a lazy smile.

'I don't know.' I am sulking. 'Having fireworks maybe or something really good.'

'Or releasing hundreds of pink and silver balloons and playing party games with them. What fun. I can hardly wait.' Ash is full of mock enthusiasm. I know he's taking the mickey out of me because I really want to go to this party and he doesn't care one way or the other. He's told me he's only coming to keep me company.

'Why don't you stay over? She's really upset that we are all leaving early.' I poke my finger into my mug of chocolate and then lick it quickly because it's still very hot.

'Jessica! Upset? What a shame,' Ash says sarcastically. 'Please, spare me any more details. It's putting me right off my food thinking about darling Jessica pining away because she's been blown out by us. Is she still able to use her hair straighteners and put on her make-up? Tell me she is. It would be such a terrible loss to the world if she let herself go.'

When I don't respond he shuts up and passes me a plate of hot buttered toast. Then he begins to eat his own toast, concentrating on it as if I'm invisible.

'It's not funny, Ash; she's really raw about it. Hey! Wait a minute. Maybe she's desperate for you to stay over because she's secretly in love with you! And that's why she's invited us. Now that would be something! What do you think?'

I am just trying to needle him, or maybe even make him laugh, anything is better than being ignored, but I am startled by his reaction. You'd think I'd really insulted him. He stops eating his toast and looks up at me with this really cold look and he's certainly not being funny now.

Ash has very distinctive eyes. Normally they are twinkly and golden brown, but now they are hard and speculative—almost irritated—like a lion surveying a prancing hyena.

'I think Jessica is just about the most stupid girl I know,' he says deliberately. And then he goes back to his toast as if it's the most fascinating thing in the world—certainly far more interesting than me.

'Sorry,' I say huffily. 'I didn't know you'd had a sense-of-humour bypass.'

'I'm bored with Jessica and her chuffing party and with you wigging off because you can't sleep over and making yourself miserable over those bloody jeans . . .' he mutters.

I am sorry then. Because he's turning his face away from me as he speaks and I know, in a rush of shame, that I must have been really irritating over the last few days if I've got on his nerves to this extent.

'Oh, none of it really matters! It's only a silly old party. I don't care if I go or not. It'll probably be really boring. And I'm taking my jeans to the Oxfam shop. It's pathetic keeping them. I'll buy some new ones . . .' I say heroically.

We eat our toast in silence. I have to force mine down because I am so unhappy. The idea that Jessica might have designs on Ash has planted itself like a rank weed in my mind. Jessica has always said she would never look twice at any lad in our year—'They are just so immature'—but Ash is different and for him she just might make an exception. I wish I hadn't said anything about her fancying him. It's a gross idea.

'I better get back,' I say miserably when I've finished my mug of chocolate. 'I promised my mother I'd have a clear-up in the spare room. Crystal and Cara are arriving on Sunday.'

'Would you like a hand?' Ash asks.

I hesitate. Mum and I have always had an unspoken rule that we never take visitors, not even best friends, upstairs. We have loads of space and a cloakroom downstairs so there has never been any need. But she broke that rule when she took Hamish MacCrimmon for a conducted tour of the house—and she even took him into the attic! He isn't even an old-established friend like Ash or Ellen. Or someone like Ralph who she has known for years. She's only just met him. Why is he so special? Just thinking about it makes me feel hurt and confused. Anyway—there is no point in fretting. Crystal and Cara will have to see upstairs. I'll just have to hope they aren't used to a posh home.

With a leap of faith I decide to trust Ash. 'Thanks, it would be a help, if you don't mind,' I say. 'It's all a bit junky upstairs . . .' I add warningly.

Ash shrugs. 'So what?'

I rabbit the whole time. It's because I'm nervous. Ash doesn't answer. I lead him upstairs, and, although I am still talking, I am watching his face. Going upstairs in our house is like walking into a time capsule. Aunt May lived in a time warp. Either that or she was very hard-up (or maybe it was both). Because nothing has been changed in the house since the 1930s—which is the time when Auntie May was a little girl. Mum says that Auntie May had an idyllic early childhood and because of that she liked to keep the house just as she remembered it.

When I was younger I accepted the fact that upstairs the curtains are so frail they have to be pulled very carefully or they come away in your hands, and that we have square rugs and old grainy wood floors rather than carpets. It didn't seem odd to me. The first time I realized that our house is strange was during my last year at junior school. We had a class visit to a museum where they showed how people lived in the past. Ellen didn't giggle, but two other girls who had visited went off into fits of laughter because the pre-war kitchen looked just like ours. We have an ancient cooker, a pot sink, a scrubbed table, and even our kettle and saucepans are period pieces. I tried not to mind the jokes: but after that I was choosy about who I took home.

On the landing I pull Ash to a halt and point to the little window. 'I can see you in your kitchen through that little pink pane . . . Look!' I command.

He is much taller than me and he has to stoop his shoulders and crouch. 'A spy in our midst,' he jokes. And as he straightens up he puts out his long arms so I am cornered. 'And do you look in on us often?'

I giggle. 'All the time, until I fall asleep with boredom. You want to make your dad do the washing up—you're rubbish at it.'

He doesn't move away. He is staring into my face. 'You don't have to watch, Rosie—you could come over.'

'I see enough of you at school—give me a break!' I joke. Anyway I am a bit embarrassed because he is looking so serious. 'My mother's a bit funny about us getting too friendly,' I add more truthfully.

'Yes, I know.'

'How do you know?'

'Well, I guessed. You keep quiet about coming to my place and you only invite me over here when she's out. You don't need to be a member of Mensa to work it out.'

'She's just worried about privacy . . . But you know, Ash, I think it would be good if your dad and my mum got to be friends.'

'Do you? Why?'

Just for a moment I am tempted to blurt out my wonderful scheme because I am used to being totally frank with Ash. The only topic I haven't aired with him is my huge crush on Joshua and my hopes for the party. So it takes an enormous effort of will-power not to tell him the truth. But I just about manage it. 'Well, we are neighbours—it would be good for them to be friends too,' I say casually. 'Come on,' I add. And I duck under his arm and grab hold of his shoulder. 'Come and see the biggest junk shop in the world.' And I run up the last of the stairs and throw open one of the heavy old doors.

I lead him into the bedroom we don't use because it has two huge fir trees in front of the windows. These trees block out all but the fiercest midsummer sun and so the room is as cold as a freezer in the winter. It is piled high with leaning towers of furniture, bric-a-brac, tin trunks, books, and tea chests. There's even an old pram and an ancient Victorian sun-lounger that has wheels and a canopy. Underneath all this, somewhere, I know there is a double bed, a chest of drawers, and a wardrobe, but all sight of them has been lost under the mountain of junk.

Ash looks around in amazement. 'Are you moving house?' he asks.

'No! It's all the stuff from the attic. The roof leaks and my mother is paranoid about all these wonderful treasures getting ruined. Every so often she goes through a trunk or a tea chest to try to clear it out. I live in hope of her finding something worth selling. But she generally ends up looking at it all, getting nostalgic, and putting it all back. Or she starts reading one of the books or looking at a photograph album and doesn't return to Planet Earth until hours later. Hopeless!'

Ash laughs. 'It's amazing, an Aladdin's cave.'

'Auntie May had a hoarding gene and my mother's got it too. Does your dad hoard?' I ask casually.

'No way,' Ash says. 'He can't bear clutter. He's kept all the photos of my mother . . . apart from that we're allowed only stuff we are actually using. Everything else is recycled or donated. He nearly has the shirts off my back before I've grown out of them . . .' Ash laughs and I try not to feel jubilant. This is confirmation that I am a genius for spotting what no one else in the world has seen—my mother and Ralph *are* the perfect match. Ralph could have hours of fun recycling this lot.

'The little girls aren't going to have to sleep in here, are they?' Ash asks. He has unearthed a glass case that contains a stuffed red squirrel and pine marten clinging to a branch. 'These beasts of the glens might just give them nightmares. I'm sure the squirrel just winked at me.'

I give him an affectionate shove. 'Don't be daft. Of course they're not going to sleep in here. It would take a week to find the bed. I just need to try to find a table for their room and maybe a lamp.'

It takes us ages because Ash keeps on finding things to look at. 'You could open an antique shop,' he says kindly. 'There're some great things in here.' He has found a parrot cage and stand. 'Who did this belong to?'

'A parrot?' I say and we both laugh. 'I really don't know,' I admit. 'Auntie May had lots of brothers. It probably belonged to one of them. They all died in World War Two. That's why she inherited the house. There's loads of their stuff here, cricket bats and clothes. She kept everything. There are boxes of letters and diaries—even their school reports. Those trunks were the ones they took away to boarding school and there are even their tuck tins somewhere. Mum keeps on saying she's going to catalogue all the papers and books. She'd need to take a sabbatical to do it, though. I think we should just have a huge bonfire and get rid of it all. I think it's morbid keeping stuff when people have died. After all, they're not going to need it again, are they?'

There is a moment of deadly silence between us. And I bite my lip, cursing my big mouth.

'Yes, that's what my father thinks,' Ash says carefully. 'He got rid of all my mother's possessions.' The merest trace of a shadow passes over Ash's face. 'Though sometimes I think I might have liked something personal of hers. Just something small—a scarf or a jumper— something she had worn—you know . . .'

'Yes, of course,' I say, as if I do know what he is talking about. Though in truth I don't understand it at all—it seems really sad, as if he's a puppy or a baby who needs a comforter.

To cover my confusion I begin to thrash around, lifting boxes and toppling piles of books. I would really like to go over to him and give him a huge hug, but although we are best friends we don't get physical and it would embarrass him if I suddenly got all touchy-feely with him. In fact it would embarrass both of us.

'Here's a lamp,' he says. 'But it's no use, it's ancient and it's only got a two-pin plug.'

'Can't we cut if off and put a square one on?' I ask.

'No, we can't!' he says. 'What were you doing in physics lessons?'

'Sleeping,' I say.

'Look, I've got a spare reading lamp. I'll bring it over for you.'

'Thanks,' I say gratefully.

'And here's a table,' he says, moving some huge plastic bags from one teetering pile to another. 'What's in these bags? They weigh a ton.'

'They're gross, like body-bags, aren't they?' I say with a shudder. Then, realizing this is another tactless remark—can't I talk about anything but death?—I add quickly, 'It's dresses and fur coats. Some of them are beautiful, all covered in beads.'

'What, the fur coats?'

'Don't be daft,' I say, laughing.

'Well, explain yourself, woman,' he says.

I give him a pretend slap for saying that. We laugh together and I stop feeling bad about being so tactless.

After the junk room, the spare room looks quite civilized. There are two single beds with iron bedsteads, an enormous wardrobe, and a lovely window that looks over the side garden and tree tops. The curtains are ancient red velvet that has faded to white where the sun hits them. Mum and I have aired the beds and made them up with clean sheets. And I've found some of my old books which I've arranged in a line on the mantelpiece along with Crystal's photo.

Ash fetches his lamp and, after we have put it on the table, the room looks complete. 'There,' I say with satisfaction. 'All ready for them.'

'You're looking forward to your cousins coming to stay, aren't you?' Ash says.

'Yes, Crystal looks so sweet in this photograph, doesn't she?'

'That was taken quite a few years ago, though, wasn't it? She looks about three. She must have changed quite a lot.'

'Yes, but she's only eleven now.' The expression on Ash's face makes me add defensively, 'Eleven year olds are lovely. You know how gorgeous the little Year Sevens are.'

'They are when they first start in the September; come Christmas some of them are real little horrors. And by Year Eight they are all monsters.'

At school Ash, Ellen, and I help run the school shop and Ash gets to deal with all the trouble makers so it's understandable that his tone is weary. But his warning annoys me. I am full of plans for the summer: my mother being a heroine and Ralph looking at her with total admiration, and us all having a lovely time with the little girls. I don't want any dire prophecies from him.

'Honestly, Ash, you're turning into a grumpy old man. First you don't want to go to Jessica's party and now you are being all gloomy about my little cousins coming to stay. Don't be such a pessimist. Tell yourself that we will have a brilliant time at the party and my cousins will be angels and it will happen. You must learn to harness positive thoughts.'

He shrugs his shoulders and looks away. The awkwardness is back between us and I don't understand it. Since the invitation to Jessica's party everything seems spoilt between us. I've got on his nerves and he on mine. At this rate we will be falling out and I'd hate that.

4

I go to Ellen's house to help her get ready for the party and by the time I have finished with her she looks gorgeous. I am so proud. She doesn't wear her glasses and she says I will have to guide her around the house because she can't see much without them.

Ellen tried contact lenses but found it stressful if they fell out because she couldn't see to find them. We've had a few times at school when practically the whole lesson has been taken up with trying to find Ellen's contact lense which was on the floor somewhere, or in her school bag, or attached to her jumper. People thought it a great time-waster—but Ellen used to get so upset I was relieved when she gave them up and went back to her glasses. I think she looks better anyway. She used to squint when she had the contacts in and she always reminded me of a little mouse that had suddenly been exposed to light.

We've been shopping and I persuaded Ellen to buy a gorgeous top that is pink and red and decorated with sequins—it's not her usual style but it really suits her. In comparison to her I look really drab. All I've got to wear is my black trousers and a black top that looks too much like a leotard to be glamorous. I bought it to double up for going out and jazz class and now I'm bored with it.

Ash comes to fetch us and to my disgust he is wearing his oldest ripped jeans and a really revolting T-shirt with a cartoon dog and Canine Defence League slogan on the front. I don't say a word: although I nearly have to superglue my mouth together to stop myself from asking him what point he is trying to make. It's just as well that Ellen is looking so stunning or we'd turn up at Jessica's party looking like the scruffy bunch.

I feel quite icy towards him, which is bad because Ralph is giving us a lift over to the party and I know I should feel grateful and warm towards Ash for organizing it.

I've never been to Jessica's house before and it's seriously smart. There's a curved driveway with signposts telling you which is the entrance and which is the exit and another sign on the circle of grass in front of the house saying *'Do not even think of parking here'*.

'How very efficient,' Ralph says admiringly.

'I think it's crass,' Ash mutters. I sigh heavily as I am fed up with him being so moody.

The house is huge and modern with an enormous garage at one side. One of the garage doors is open and I can see the shadowy shapes of people inside. 'Oh, the party's in the garage—how cool!' I say.

'Out you get. Have a good time,' Ralph says briskly. He's obviously allowed two minutes in his busy schedule to drop us off and he doesn't want us hanging about in the car gawping at the grandness of Jessica's house and feeling shy.

'Come on, then,' I say a tad impatiently to the others.

I pull Ellen out of the car and link arms with her because she's making little mewing noises under her breath—like a lost kitten.

'Hush now,' I croon in a whisper. 'I won't abandon you.'

We make our way slowly over towards the garage. Ellen is gripping on to me as if I'm her keeper and Ash looks as if he has toothache. His face is positively sulky. We must look like a bunch of weirdos.

Jessica hurries out of the garage and holds out her arms to us. For a moment I wonder if she is going to give us a collective hug, but then she starts to shepherd us towards the front door.

'Josh is just sorting out some music in there. Nothing that we want to be bothered with,' she says, smiling. 'Come on into the house, everything is ready.'

I can't help but feel puzzled because I got a glimpse of the inside of the garage before she turned us away and it certainly looked as if a party was starting in there. I saw boxes of beer on the floor and the shadowy shapes of bodies and in the background was the dull thud of music.

Inside the house the hallway is decorated with balloons and streamers. 'The cloakroom is here,' Jessica says, pointing to one of the many doors leading off the hall. Everything in the house is so bright I feel I need sunglasses. I've never seen so much white glossy paint and gleaming new wood in the whole of my life.

'The dining room is for dancing; there's a lovely parquet floor.' Jessica flips open the door for us. 'The other rooms are out of bounds but the kitchen is huge for chillin' in and there's a load to eat and drink. Come on in. There's a great friend of yours here too, Rose,' Jessica adds.

'Really?' I say with surprise.

The kitchen is empty. I look along the frosted marble worktops and marvel at the number of stainless steel gadgets and electrical contraptions Jessica's mother has. I have no idea what most of them do, but they really look impressive, rather like the inside of a space shuttle.

'Who is here?' I ask politely. Both my best friends are with me and no one else from our year at school has been invited.

'Mrs Waugh.' Jessica gives me a slow Cheshire-cat-type smile. 'She's house-sitting this weekend. She lives in the village and is my mother's general help. But of course you'd know all about that, wouldn't you, Rose? Mrs Waugh's always talking about you and singing your praises.'

'That's nice,' I say brightly. 'Mrs Waugh is one of the mothers at dancing and she helps with the chaperoning at shows so I know her pretty well. But I didn't know she worked for your mother or was your house-sitter.'

'Of course, we don't really need a house-sitter. But my mother fusses so. You will be careful, won't you? No drinks or mess in the dining room,' Jessica says, smiling at Ash.

He scowls and mutters, 'Speaking strictly for myself I think I'm just about house-trained—it is several years since I last crapped my pants.'

Ellen giggles but my face is frosty.

'I'll be back in a minute,' Jessica says, just as if he had not spoken. And the three of us are left alone in the kitchen.

'Isn't it just the loveliest house you've ever seen?' Ellen says politely, gazing around the kitchen like a prospective buyer, and blinking in the fierce glow from the many spotlights that beam in from the ceiling.

Ash makes a dismissive noise in his throat and begins to eat the food that has been laid out on the table.

Mrs Waugh comes in from a utility room—her arms full of fragrant piles of ironing. 'Oh, you're here, Rose, love! Thank goodness for that. I kept on saying to Jessie, is anyone ever coming to this party when I've got all this food ready? I was getting quite worried for her—she's worked all day getting the house looking nice.'

'There are some more people in the garage,' I say helpfully.

'They're sorting out some music,' Ellen adds.

'Oh lovely,' Mrs Waugh says. 'Will there be some dancing?' She laughs as she adds, 'You'll get them going, won't you, Rose?'

She disappears off with the ironing. And Ash mutters to me in a disagreeable tone, 'Don't say you've been invited along as the star turn! I don't think I can bear it.'

I ignore him. I love parties. I feel quite light-headed with excitement. I want to dance and drink punch and talk nonsense with Joshua. I want to have a really good

33

time and I don't want Ash moping around and being grumpy and spoiling it for me. I turn my back on him and inspect the drinks. There's lots of stuff that looks as if it might be alcohol, but isn't. There is no sign of any punch—I feel a little frisson of disappointment.

Mrs Waugh comes back and whispers to me, 'The girls are here with me; I had to bring them along because their dad is on nights this week. Could they pop down and see you before anyone else arrives? They're that excited that you're here.'

'Yes, that would be lovely,' I say. I join Ash at the table covered with food. 'There are two little girls from my dancing school here. They are in one of the classes I help with, and they are coming down to see me. Do try to be pleasant,' I add rather plaintively. He takes absolutely no notice of me—which I hate. I can cope with anything but being ignored.

I'm not ignored for long. Gemma and Katie rush into the kitchen and hurl themselves at me, swinging on my hands and hugging me until I feel quite dizzy. 'Promise you'll be our chaperone this year during the show?' Gemma begs.

'And promise you'll write some more stories for us. We want you to be our chaperone every day,' Katie says.

'Well, I don't know,' I say laughing at them. 'I haven't fixed the schedules yet with Mrs Valente. But I'll see what I can do. I'm going to be very busy because I've got my two little cousins coming to stay with me and they are going to be in the show.'

'Are they staying with you all summer?' Katie asks. 'Are they going on holiday with you too? Lucky them . . .'

'Yes, they're staying all summer, but no, we're not going on holiday. I'm too busy really, with the show and everything.'

I haven't told anyone the truth, not even Ash, that Mum has said that even with the money Milo has promised to send for the two little girls there is still no way we could afford to go away on holiday this year, not even camping or staying in really cheap places.

'We live in such a lovely house we don't need to go on holiday. And we'll be too busy anyway, with Crystal and Cara. I don't mind,' I said to Mum. But the truth is I mind dreadfully and am getting hacked off with hearing about everyone else's holiday plans. Ash and Ralph are going sailing, and even that sounds like a riot compared to staying at home. Not even rehearsals and the show will fill the whole of the holidays. And I know that everyone else will come back in September with fabulous tans and endless stories of the great time they had. Jessica is sure to have the usual sick-making photos of a wonderful looking boy rubbing sun oil into her back and drooling over her. She's been having mind-boggling holiday romances since Year Seven. Eventually, by the time she is thirty, she will have a boyfriend in every country of the world all sending her cuddly toys and letters and wanting to marry her.

'I wish I was your cousin,' Katie says, pressing her face against my arm, and that cheers me up no end.

'Mam's got the music from *Grease*. Will you teach us some of the dances? We came to see the afternoon show you did at your school. We thought you were the best Sandy ever,' Gemma says, pressing her face against my other arm.

'Oh, I don't know . . .' I say. I would love to dance with them, they are so sweet. But I am terrified of Josh coming into the room and finding me making an idiot of myself.

'Please, please, please,' they chorus.

'Look, no one's here yet,' Ellen says. 'We may as well do something. It'll be fun.'

'There are people here,' I whisper to her. 'They're in the garage.'

Anyway there seems no point in arguing. So we all

go into the dining room. It has the most amazing floor. The wood gleams with polish and a huge space in the middle has been cleared for dancing. I have to stop myself from breaking into a polka at the sight of it. Just as we are getting the CD player sorted Jessica comes in followed by a lanky brown-haired boy.

'Hi!' the lanky boy says to Ellen.

'Hi,' she replies and blushes red as a beetroot.

'Who's that?' I whisper.

'Jessica's brother.'

'Really?'

'Her younger brother. He goes to our church. He's . . .'

I lose the rest of what she is going to say because Jessica is being all wild and enthusiastic about us doing some numbers from *Grease*. I can't help but feel flattered. 'Reece,' she commands the lanky boy. 'Come and join in and dance with Ellen. Rose is going to show everyone how to jive. It'll be good fun.'

It is fun. Ash refuses to dance—what a surprise. But Reece and Ellen make a pair and Jessica and I jitterbug with the two little ones. They are lovely and light for throwing around. We dance for ages until we are all breathless and laughing—apart from Ash who sits by the window watching us with cold amber eyes like a malevolent tom-cat.

Eventually Mrs Waugh says it's time for the girls to go to bed, and after lots of hugging and fuss they disappear. When I turn around I find that the garage shadows are slowly coming into the house. They drift in to eat food and grab Cokes in twos and threes. One strange thing I notice is that all the boys are wearing dark blue jeans and grey hoodies and the girls are all wearing black skirts and white tops—like waitresses. Most odd.

Mrs Waugh pops her head around the kitchen door and is pleased to see that people are here and most of the food has been eaten.

'There—I haven't been an old killjoy, have I?' she says to Jessica.

'No,' Jessica beams. 'It's been lovely. Everyone is in the dining room dancing.'

'Well, I knew Rose would get the party going with a swing,' Mrs Waugh says with satisfaction.

In fact there aren't many people in the dining room at all, only about two or three couples, and there is still no sign of Josh. He must be in the garage. I bet they're having much more fun in there with booze and loud music. I feel depressed suddenly. Jessica has disappeared now and I don't know any of the people in the dining room apart from Ash (who is ignoring me) and Ellen and Reece who are still dancing together.

I go back to the kitchen and check the clock in there. It's ages until there's even the remotest chance of Ellen's parents coming to collect us. This is awful. I wish I'd offered to read Gemma and Katie a bedtime story—at least it would have been something to do.

'Hi. Have I missed all the fun?'

I spin round. Josh too is wearing a grey hoodie and dark jeans but looks heaps better than all the other boys. His blond hair is dark with gel and his face unshaven; a faint golden shadow shimmers on his cheeks. He is utterly gorgeous and I have to peel my eyes away from him and concentrate on the floor for fear I am staring like a love-sick puppy.

'What fun are you talking about?' I ask, risking a sideways glance.

'I heard you were a star,' Josh says, grinning. This is an eerie echo of Ash's words earlier in the evening: 'Don't tell me you've been invited along as the star turn . . .' and I feel awkward. In the back of my mind is an unhappy thought trying to surface. I won't face it. I refuse to think about anything but the fact that I am alone in a room with Joshua and he is talking to me. This is nothing short of miraculous. All my daydreams about him have started just like this. I should be as happy as a lamb in clover. I curse myself for feeling so ill-at-ease.

'I don't have a clue what you are talking about. I did a bit of dancing with Mrs Waugh's little girls, that's all.' I walk over to the table and start to attack a bowl of crisps manically.

He laughs and joins me at the table. He's standing a bit too close to me for total comfort. I hope he doesn't notice that my hands are shaking and realize being near to him is making me fall apart at the seams. We eat the crisps together. But when it gets to the last one he snatches it and leans across to feed it to me. It would be really romantic apart from the fact that my mouth feels like the Sahara—dry as a bone from salt and monosodium glutamate. And I can't get over to the drinks table without pushing him away. He's got me boxed in by perching on the edge of the table and putting his foot on the cupboard opposite. I bet his mother would go mad to see his big dirty trainer on her lovely white wood door.

'Excuse me,' I mumble. 'I need a drink.'

I edge closer to his leg, expecting him to let me through, but instead he grabs my arm and pulls me against him. 'Come out to the garage and have a proper drink. Old War and Peace doesn't have a clue about what we've got out there.'

'OK,' I say.

He runs his hands down the length of my back like a racehorse trainer checking out a filly. It makes me shudder.

'You're neat,' he says. 'I wish I'd seen you strutting your stuff. Jess says you were great. Come and have a dance in the garage with the big boys.' His tone is mocking. His head dips and I know a kiss is coming. I duck away from him. There is no way I am kissing Joshua Browne with a mouth reeking of cheese-and-onion and lips like sandpaper. (Oh-my-goodness-why-did-I-eat-those-crisps?) I've dreamt about this minute for so long.

I am determined for it to be perfect. I am so thrilled he's invited me out to the garage I feel like crying from happiness. But the thing I need most in the world is a glass of water.

'See you out there then,' he says. He isn't looking at me and there is a dismissive tone in his voice. But then, as if to make up for this, his hand traces a path down my spine again and he slaps my bum—just one sharp playful tap—but I leap away from him as if his hand is on fire. I try to tell myself that this is really cool, but the truth is I don't like being slapped like that. It's as if I am an old cow at market. In my daydreams Joshua is gentle and loving. I am getting a bad dose of reality.

Once I am alone in the kitchen I gulp down two glasses of cold water. Then I get my handbag and rush off to the cloakroom. When I look in the mirror I find my hair is wild, a frizz of blonde curls, and my cheeks are flushed. I sigh and splash my face with cold water. Then I put on some kohl eye pencil and lip gloss and tell myself to calm down.

I leave by the back door to give myself a bit of time, and walk around to the garage very slowly. I straighten my spine, do deep breathing, and get myself centred, like I do before I go on stage. I am determined to be cool, calm, and collected by the time I get into the garage to strut my stuff. If darling Joshua wants to see me dance I will be like the little girl in *The Red Shoes*, nothing will stop me.

Because I am coming from the back of the house I approach the garage along a little path that divides it from the house. Josh and one of the hoodies are standing at the top of this path sharing a cigarette. Pungent blue smoke surrounds them like an aura at a seance. They are busy puffing, and my thin-soled shoes make no sound on the flags, so they don't realize I am behind them. I am just about to tap Josh on the arm when Hoodie says with a laugh, 'So which one did you pull? The goofy one or the one with no tits?'

All I register is Josh's laugh—a coarse blokey sound. I turn round and run back the way I have come, my hand over my mouth to stop any sound.

I stand panting by the back door. Poor Ellen with her brace and me with my dancer's physique—we are just figures of fun. They don't care that Ellen has the sweetest nature in the world and is the best friend anyone could wish for. All they see are the external things. I tell myself that boys like Josh and Hoodie are shallow and not worth bothering with. And I try not to care—I remind myself that I am lucky to be a 32AA when I wear a leotard and leap across a dance floor. No one wants big tits then, do they? But I can't stop tears of hurt filling my eyes.

I stay on the back doorstep for ages; feeling sorry for myself, feeling angry, feeling glad that I didn't let Josh kiss me. And then feeling disappointed because now I will never know what it would have been like. I dash hot tears from my eyes and chew my lips until finally all emotion leaves me and I feel totally tired and miserable. I've been nursing my crush on Joshua for weeks now. I'm lost without it.

Ash puts his head round the door. 'Oh, you're here, are you? We thought you'd gone out to the garage.'

'No—why should I go out there?' I snap.

'I don't know. Isn't that where all the action is?' Ash asks.

'I don't know,' I say irritably. 'I just got hot. I wanted some fresh air.'

'Are you OK, Rosie?' he asks. He comes out of the back door and stands in front of me, looking down into my face.

'Yes,' I say, avoiding his eyes and wishing I sounded more certain. I hate keeping secrets from Ash. Things are always better when I talk them over with him. But having a broken heart and a flat chest are not topics I feel I can air with him right now.

'Most people are in the dining room now. Do you want

to come and have a dance? I mean if you don't mind dancing with me. I mean, it's couples and I don't want to dance with anyone but you.'

'OK,' I say. 'But, by the way, how big are your feet? Size thirteen? That's a very unlucky number. You will be very careful not to maim me, won't you?'

We are laughing when we go into the dining room. But I am pulled up short by the sight of Josh snogging one of the girls in waitress uniform and Ellen and Reece smooching like a pair of lovers. There is no sign of Jessica.

It's a relief to grab hold of Ash and disappear into the crowd. He is tall enough to hide all things from my eyes. I lose myself against the dog on his T-shirt and concentrate on the music.

We dance for ages and then go into the kitchen to get a drink. Jessica's there, sitting on the table, drinking a can of Coke. She's obviously been supping something stronger in the garage because her eyes are slightly glazed and her speech is very deliberate as if she is determined not to slur her words.

'I thought you didn't like dancing?' she says to Ash, her voice tart as unsweetened rhubarb. 'Change your mind?'

'Yeah,' he says.

'Why don't you just pull her and get it over with?' she says with a sneer.

'Why don't you mind your own bloody business,' Ash says, his voice no more than an icy whisper. Somehow Ash speaking quietly is scarier than most people shouting.

Jessica jumps down and flounces from the room.

'What was all that about? Did she want you to dance with her?' I ask suspiciously. 'And who does she think you should pull?'

'She asked me to dance,' Ash mumbles. 'I told her I wasn't a performing bloody bear. Stuck up bloody cow.'

'Ash! Don't be so rude! We are at her house! But who does she think you should pull?' I ask again.

'Nobody . . .' Ash says defensively. His face is flushed and moody.

'All the girls here are in Josh's year so they're heaps older than you,' I say primly.

'So . . . Reece is Year Eight but it isn't stopping Ellen.'

'YEAR EIGHT! Oh-my-goodness-that-is-truly-terrible! Does Ellen know?'

'I suppose so. He seems a decent enough lad.'

'But Ellen will never live this down at school! We are going to be Year Eleven when we go back.'

'So? He'll be Year Nine,' Ash says coolly.

'Oh-my-goodness-we-have-got-to-do-something-about-this!' I am just about to rush from the room, and rescue Ellen from this fate worse than death, when Ash grabs hold of my hand and stops me.

'Calm your ponies, Rose, and get a grip! You are not Ellen's minder. If she wants to pull a lad who's younger than us it's her lookout, not yours—don't be such a control freak.'

'But think what people will say! I suppose you think it's all right because you've been chatting up some older girl,' I add accusingly.

'Shut your big mouth!' he says angrily. 'And Ellen's parents will be here any minute so just leave her alone. She never has any fun and she's enjoying herself this evening.'

His angry tone chills me. I pull my hand away from his and go over to the sink for a glass of water so he will not see the tears in my eyes. I can't believe he is being so horrible. This has been a truly hateful evening.

5

I wake to the sound of crying. For a few moments I think I am still asleep. My night has been plagued by terrors when I dreamt I was lost in a forest, searching for Ash and unable to find him. And for a split second I think the crying is the sound of my own despair.

Then I realize, with relief, that I am dry-eyed and cold grey light is streaming through the gap in my curtains. When I hop out of bed I make a grab for my fleece jacket because the day not only looks cold—it is cold—one of those wild summer mornings when the wind veers from the north and an arctic chill descends on County Durham.

Shivering, I follow the sound of crying. It leads me to the kitchen. Mum is there, in her dressing gown. The cooker is alight, with the door propped open, so the kitchen is marginally less chilly than the rest of the house. Sitting at the table are two girls. My cousins have arrived! The smaller of the two—Cara—is sobbing. Crystal is sitting next to her, not doing anything, just sitting. And the first thing I notice is the complete stillness of her. It's as if she's a statue. The next thing I notice, to my horror, is her hair. It is long, very long, reaching well down her back and is dark as night. It also has ghastly purple and gold highlights in it—like a psychedelic zebra.

Slowly she turns her head to look at me. She has very dark upswept eyes. In the photo when she was a little girl her eyes were smiley and cute—like blackcurrents. Now they are as hard as slivers of jet.

'Hi!' I say, with what I hope is enthusiasm. 'You must

be Crystal and Cara. Sorry I wasn't here to welcome you. I was out at a party till late . . .' I stop abruptly. Those dark eyes are looking at me with such ill-concealed contempt that I realize only too late how idiotic all this sounds. Of course they are Crystal and Cara and nobody in the world cares that I was partying.

'Cara isn't very well. She's been sick . . .' Mum says anxiously.

'And she's got a rash, it's all over her belly,' Crystal says, giving Mum a sly sideways glance.

'Oh dear, what did your father say about it?'

'He said it was heat rash,' Crystal says with grim satisfaction.

'Well, it's certainly not heat rash today, it's freezing,' I say, making my way over to the cooker and warming my hands. Mum hands me a mug of tea and I take it gratefully.

'I really need some Calpol or something,' Mum says, looking distracted. At that moment Cara starts to make choking noises and Mum dashes her over to the sink. I look down at my tea and try to hide my disgust.

'Maybe she should be in bed,' I say.

'I need to find out what is the matter with her,' Mum replies. 'There, there, poor poppet,' she adds gently to Cara, as she lifts her up and wipes her face with a flannel.

'Maybe it's travel sickness,' I say helpfully. 'Do you remember how Ellen used to throw up all day after she'd been on a long journey, especially if it was a coach? In the end she had to have hypnotherapy to brainwash her out of it.'

'Cara's never sick in the car,' Crystal snaps at me—as if I'd said something really stupid. I'm beginning to wish I'd stayed in bed.

Mum sits Cara down at the table and she immediately starts howling again. Her little face is all red and hot looking. Mum looks just about ready to burst into tears herself.

'Well, what did Milo have to say about it?' I ask Mum, ignoring a sharp look from Crystal when I mention his name. 'He must have realized she was ill.'

'He was in a hurry. He just dropped the girls off and left. I suppose he thought it would be better that way. He can't have realized . . .' Mum says, avoiding my eyes.

'Was she sick in the car?' I ask Crystal.

'No!' she snaps in reply. But I know she is lying.

'I suppose he'll be on his way to the airport by now. No help there then,' I say in a resigned voice. It's funny the way Uncle Milo and trouble always seem to go together.

Mum holds Cara close to her and strokes the damp dark hair back from her face. Mum looks terrified. I don't remember her panicking like this when I was little and ill. I suppose I never cried in the terrible heartbroken way that Cara is.

'I think I am going to have to ask Ralph if he will pop over and have a look at her,' Mum says. 'I can't leave her like this.'

'Oh, Mum—you can't do that,' I say. Mum's hair is a wild tangle and she's wearing a candlewick dressing gown that once belonged to Auntie May. It's so old it's threadbare in places and it's impossible to know what colour it was originally. It's the kind of ragged old thing that never looks clean even when it's just been washed; and now, thanks to Cara, it's got all sorts down the front: tea and snot and tears—and probably a lot worse.

'You go and get dressed and I'll clear up the kitchen. Then we could take Cara down to the doctor together,' I say reasonably.

'There's no surgery on a Sunday,' Mum says desperately. 'There's nothing else for it. I'll ring Ralph before he goes out jogging and ask him to pop in.'

'Mum, you can't do that. He's a consultant gynaecologist. He doesn't do sick kids,' I say a bit desperately. The kitchen looks and smells like a hell hole.

And no one would ever want to marry a woman who wears a dressing gown like the one Mum's got on.

'I'll just run across the courtyard and ask him,' Mum says. 'I'll have to be quick. You know how prompt he is. You keep an eye on . . .'

'I'll go,' I say in a resigned voice. Compared to Mum my pyjama bottoms and fleece look like a fashion statement. At that moment Crystal smirks. She wipes the smile off her face immediately when she realizes I am looking at her and gives me a blank look. But not before I'd seen that smirk. She's enjoying the fact that Mum is upset and I am running around in my night clothes. Our lives are being totally disrupted and they've only been in the house a matter of minutes. Why should that please her? For a second I am totally shocked, and then I am angry. Then Cara starts howling so loudly that I bolt out of the door and fetch Ralph at a run. I just want this all to be over as quickly and painlessly as possible. Like the party last night everything this morning is horrible, horrible, horrible and I can't see how anything will ever make it better.

Ralph and Ash are just coming out of their door as I cross the yard. I'm not sure if this is a blessing or not. They are both wearing vests and running shorts and well-scrubbed trainers. I try not to look at the vast expanse of hairy legs on show. Living with just Mum has made me shy about things like that. I am also reminded, painfully, of being pressed up against the dog on Ash's T-shirt last night. I find myself blushing.

Looking at the ground I mutter, 'Cara, my little cousin who has come to stay, is being sick, she's got a rash, and my mother is worried.'

I hardly have time to get the words out. 'I'll put a tracksuit on and I'll be over in a minute,' Ralph says, and he disappears inside.

'Are you OK?' Ash asks me. I am studying the tubs of blue and white flowers that stand guard by their door as if I have suddenly developed an overwhelming interest in horticulture.

'Yes,' I say miserably.

'It is bad luck that your little cousin is ill. But don't worry, Dad will get her sorted. He's a great doctor, you know.'

'Yes,' I say again.

'I'm sorry about the party,' he says. 'I kind of knew that snotty Jessica was setting us up for a sting, but I couldn't suss out how it would work before we got there. We were like the three stooges, weren't we? The perfect smokescreen to hide the real action in the garage. Presumably that's why she wanted us to stay over.'

'What?' I say.

'There were loads of people in the garage—I went out there to look for you and found a whole alternative party—and they all dressed the same so they could take it in turns to come into the house and Mrs Waugh wouldn't work out what was going on.'

I stare at him, my mouth gaping.

'Surely you'd worked it out?' he says. Then, as he studies my face, he mutters to himself, 'Oh, shit . . .'

'We're not all blessed with your fantastic brain—' I say bitterly. 'And I didn't go out to the garage so no, I hadn't worked it out. But thank you so much for enlightening me.'

But I should have known. The uncomfortable thought I kept ignoring when Joshua was talking to me was the realization that I had been set up. I just didn't want to believe it.

'I thought Joshua was . . . I heard Jessica say to him . . . I thought . . .' Ash mumbles.

'What did she say? And what did you think?'

'Oh nothing . . .' he says gruffly, and turns away. He suddenly seems to have turned into a big ginger Neanderthal with furry legs. He can't seem to put a sentence together.

47

'Ash! Come here and tell me,' I say warningly.

He turns back and scuffs the toe of his trainer against the tub of little flowers. 'Jessica told Joshua he had to dance with you and she kept making jokes about you fancying him.' Ash kicks at the tub quite viciously.

We can hear Ralph in the kitchen. I turn away.

Ash's voice is just a whisper. 'Well, do you?'

I turn back to him; his face is stern and unsmiling. 'Do I what?' I ask.

'Fancy Joshua . . .'

'Oh, please, he's such a slime-ball,' I say with exaggerated weariness. Ash doesn't smile. I thought he might. He just looks away.

'Come on, then. Let's see the patient,' Ralph says, and he walks across the courtyard so quickly I have to almost run to keep up.

Ralph is an absolute hero. No woman could see him in his doctor role and not fall in love with him immediately. It cheers me up no end because Mum is sure to be besotted after this!

He sits Cara on his knee, brave man that he is, and talks to her as if she is grown-up and sensible instead of being a four-year-old sick bag. He asks if he can lift her little top to look at her tummy and, after he has peeked at her rash, he says: 'You've eaten something that doesn't agree with you. It's an allergy rash. Did you have something unusual for supper last night?'

She nods her head and almost manages a smile. 'We went out for a meal, with Daddy. I had octopus and strawberries and all sorts of things. And it was the middle of the night,' she says delightedly.

'Dad was late home. We had a celebration meal with him,' Crystal says defensively.

'Well, hives doesn't explain the sickness or the temperature,' Ralph says kindly. 'So let me see if we can find out what is making you feel so poorly.' He then looks in Cara's ears and tells us she has an ear infection and needs an antibiotic. He takes out his mobile and rings someone called Keith (who turns out to be our doctor) and arranges for a prescription to be faxed to the duty chemist. Then, wonderful man, he goes off in his car to fetch it. While he is out we dash around, getting washed and dressed and clearing up the kitchen. Then Cara has her medicine, is wrapped in a blanket and propped in a chair. She seems loads better already and almost human.

My one moment of worry comes when Ralph says to Mum, 'Give this little one lots of fluids and keep her warm.' And he adds, 'You'll need the heating on today—it's like winter.' And I hold my breath. I desperately don't want Mum to tell him that the boiler has packed up. He doesn't appear to have noticed that the house is a tip—he has been concentrating on Cara. And maybe when he's in doctor mode he doesn't register other things.

'Yes, I'll light the fire in the sitting room straightaway,' Mum says, pushing her hair out of her eyes in a way she does when she is worried.

'I'll do it,' I say eagerly.

'If you need any shopping just give us a shout. I'll send Ashley over for the list and we'll pop down in the car.'

'Thank you so much,' Mum says gratefully.

They smile at each other. And if this was a Hollywood film there would be a rising swell of music in the background and the camera would linger on Ralph looking into my mother's eyes. And, after he has left, my mother would shake her head with a little sigh and a single violin would wail. It is lovely pretending it's all happening inside my head. It's quite a disappointment when I realize that he's left and Mum is peeling potatoes for lunch and doesn't seem at all interested in talking about how wonderful Ralph is.

'Yes, he's very kind and competent, isn't he?' she says vaguely. I then notice that although she has managed to get dressed in some clean jeans she is wearing odd socks.

It drives me nuts when she does things like that. I hate things not matching. Ralph is the last person on the planet who would wear odd socks, so I bet it would drive him nuts too. I sigh and try not to feel irritable.

I decide that after I have got the sitting room fire going I will go through my mother's sock drawer and sort it out. Hopefully Ralph will now be a regular visitor and I don't want him being put off by my mother's bizarre dressing habits.

When the fire is roaring (I'm good at fires) Mum moves Cara into the sitting room and offers to switch the TV on for her. 'I'm not sure what will be on . . .' Mum says lamely; she never watches television so she wouldn't know.

'We don't have a video or Sky,' I say to Crystal, and I wince at the expression of horror on her face. Of course, there's nothing they want to watch. 'Rose has lots of lovely books,' Mum says smiling.

'I'll sort them out, don't worry,' I say to Mum. I find Cara a colouring book and get my artist pencils from my school bag.

'I hate reading,' Crystal says, frowning at the pile of books I produce. She gets a Game Boy out of her duffle bag and curls up in a chair with that. I am diplomatic and don't point out that a book might be more interesting.

I can't face sitting in the same room as Cara and Crystal. The sight of them hurts my eyes. Crystal isn't like a little girl at all—she is as hard faced and confident as someone of about twenty. She makes me feel immature and stupid—as if I am the younger one. Cara might be all right when she's well but at the moment she smells awful. Mum has said something about a bath for her later on. Without the boiler we have only an elderly immersion heater which takes hours and hours to produce anything remotely warm. This is fine on a boiling hot day—when a tepid bath is refreshing—but not good on a day like today. Goodness knows how we are going to manage if the weather stays like this. I shall have to ask Ash if I can have a shower when Ralph goes out.

I go up to Mum's room, and ring Ellen on the extension. We have a code. I let the phone ring three times and then hang up and Ellen phones me back. Ellen's dad is an executive with a multi-national and he doesn't mind huge phone bills. I snuggle under Mum's eiderdown and get ready for a good long chat.

'How was church?' I ask.

'Wonderful,' Ellen says. I then get a minute by minute description of the morning service and coffee afterwards. I don't mind this because Ellen and her family go to an American Gospel church and it's very noisy and fun with guitars and drums and lots of happy songs.

A couple of years back Mum did a cycle of poems about religion. And for her research we went to every different kind of church, synagogue, mosque, temple, and stone circle you could think of. I loved it because although I was twelve I looked loads younger and everyone always made a big fuss of me.

My favourites were the Quakers (because you can sit and daydream) and the Spiritualists because you get cool messages from the other side. The visiting spirits don't tell you winning lottery numbers or anything like that—just cosy stuff—but I used to enjoy it no end. One of the mediums told me she could see my spirit guide and he was a Native American chief called Silver Eagle. Even Ash was impressed by that! (Although he tried to hide it by making silly jokes about how my guide should be called 'Rainbow Chaser'—because my head is full of impossible schemes—or 'Babbling Brook' as I talk all the time.)

This morning it's Ellen who is doing all the talking. Finally she stops and I have the chance to ask, 'Was Reece Browne at church?'

'Yes,' she says.

'It's a long way for him to go.'

'He gets a lift over with Penfold and his family. He's really lovely, isn't he, Rosie?' she asks happily.

I am diplomatic and don't answer. I feel pretty mean towards all the Browne family this morning. I hate being taken for a ride.

'Did you work out that we'd been invited to the party solely as a decoy to keep Mrs Waugh happy?' I ask rather bitterly. 'And Jessica asked her brothers to get off with us to keep us sweet.'

'Oh no!' Ellen sounds genuinely upset.

'Ellen! You'll have to face it. Jessica set us up. Or rather she set me up. I suppose she thinks I'm like some clockwork doll; wind me up and it's instant entertainment.'

'I'm sure it wasn't like that, Rose. She invited you because you're such good fun. Look at the great time we had, dancing and everything. I had the best time ever . . .' she adds wistfully.

'I suppose she thinks I can be relied on to show off,' I say miserably. 'But I think it's absolutely awful of her to set us up with her brothers.'

'Oh, Rose, that is such a negative thing to say. I'm sure it wasn't like that.'

'Well, you heard her command Reece to dance with you, and Ash heard her telling Joshua to dance with me. He asked me to go out to the garage but I didn't. I think he's a real slimy pillock.'

'But, Rosie, I thought you liked him . . .'

'Well, I don't.'

'I can't believe that Reece would . . . you know . . . dance with me and everything and make me feel so special just because Jessica told him to,' Ellen says sadly.

'ELLEN! You can't have a crush on him!' I squawk. 'He's a Year Eight. You'll be the talk of the school if people find out you're getting together with him.'

'Rose, that's ridiculous, what difference does age make? I'm the youngest person in our year and Reece is very mature. It really doesn't matter—does it?' Ellen asks uncertainly.

'Oh, Ellen, of course it does! It will matter like mad at school if anyone finds out. Believe me.'

'Rosie, please listen. I liked him before the party. We've chatted after church a few times and he's a really genuine person.'

'Ellen!' I say warningly. 'Remember. He danced with you because his sister told him to.'

'I suppose so,' Ellen says sadly.

'I'm not talking to Jessica. And if you've got any sense you'll blow Reece out too. Stupid little Year Eight—goodness, Ellen—he's hardly out of short trousers.'

'Yes,' Ellen says. But she doesn't sound totally convinced.

We talk about other things for a bit, but the party and her feelings for Reece have cast a shadow over our chat. We arrange to meet the next day and hang up.

Reluctantly, I go down to the sitting room. Crystal and Cara are both fast asleep. Crystal is clutching her Game Boy to her, with her face cushioned against the arm of the chair. It doesn't look very comfortable—she must be really tired to sleep like that. She looks better now; her face is softer, and her cupid-bow mouth curves in a little smile.

It's the first chance I've had to study her; looking straight at her when she's awake is like facing up to a bad-tempered dog—it's best to avoid eye contact. I can't believe that everything about her is so grown-up: the hair dye, the trendy clothes, the smudges of mascara under her eyes. It's difficult to believe she's really only eleven. She's tall as well, only a couple of inches shorter than me and thin as a whippet. Even the hand clutching the Nintendo is bony.

I sigh. She couldn't be any more different to the little smiling girl in the cygnet costume, or the charming child of my imagination. My only consolation is that my plan for Mum and Ralph seems to be progressing at a speed that is nothing short of miraculous and that cheers me up.

I am humming a tune and doing a little dance as I go into the kitchen. But I am pulled up short by the sight of my mother, leaning against the boiler and reading aloud from her manuscript of poems. This is no good! Ralph will never fall in love with her properly if she persists in being so eccentric. First odd socks—now this!

'Mum!' I say loudly.

'Oh, darling, you're here,' she says.

It's then that I see the legs: dark blue, jean-covered legs. Someone—a man—is lying on the floor next to the boiler while my mother reads aloud to him. Oh-my-goodness-this-is-getting-worse!

'Mum. What are you doing?'

'I'm reading my new poem to Hamish. He has very kindly come over to have a tinker with the boiler and he thinks he can get it going. Isn't that wonderful?'

'It's probably only a fuse or something small. You should have got Ralph to have a look at it when he was here earlier,' I say sulkily.

'Rose, he's a gynaecologist, not a plumber,' Mum says.

There's a guffaw of laughter from the other side of the boiler and my face reddens. I hate being laughed at. I go up to my room and sulk. I suppose Hamish MacCrimmon will be staying for lunch. Damn and blast!

Curling up in bed is no fun at all. My daydreams about Joshua are all spoilt. There is nothing about him that I like any more. I find myself thinking about Ash and hoping he will not be grumpy with me now the party is over. I think about dancing with him. He is always surprising me. I didn't know he knew how to dance . . . He's a sly fox; he's probably been pulling girls for years and not telling me and Ellen about it.

That thought makes me feel terrible. I don't like to think of Ash having secrets that I don't know about. I want to believe that we are totally honest with each other and can talk about anything and everything. A little voice in my head reminds me that I deliberately didn't tell him about my crush on Joshua . . . Or my plans for our parents. Why was that? I ask myself. But I don't want to think about it, or go down that road.

I leap out of bed and change quickly into my practice clothes, with some good thick leg warmers. Then I race down to the dining room and begin a warm-up. It works—soon I am not thinking about anything but the imaginary music in my head—and the wonderful release that comes from making my body do what I want it to.

6

Ellen is depressed during the last week of term. Stress always makes her ill so she has constant headaches and tummy pains. I suspect she's unhappy about the party, although I can't get her to admit it.

Whenever I try to talk about what a fiasco it was she gives me a sad patient smile and says: 'Oh, no, Rosie! Don't say that! It wasn't terrible. I had the best time ever.' She reminds me of a suffering Brontë sister or some tragic Victorian heroine and I am desperate to cheer her up.

Ash is no help; at any mention of Jessica—or the party—he just raises his eyes to heaven and makes some stupid joke. Jessica is cutting us all dead—we are invisible to her. This should be a relief as it saves any unpleasantness—but for some reason it really irritates me. I wanted us to ignore her—not the other way round.

To make it all a million times worse Reece haunts us. I had no idea who the hell he was until I met him at the party—so I can't believe that he has always been such a presence in our lives.

But now . . . wherever we turn he seems to be there: the school shop, the bus queue, the library, the vending machine. He seems to have some kind of sixth sense as to where we are going to be next, and like a bad smell he turns up. And every time we see him we have to go through the same stupid charade of pleasantness.

'Hi, Ellen,' he says, locking on to her like a surface-to-air missile. He then mutters 'Hello' to the rest of us.

We ignore him—he's a Year Eight twit after all. But

Ellen, with her kind heart, bless her, always says, 'Hello, Reece! How are you doing?' And if we are not careful it turns into a proper conversation. Ellen is stuck there with him, her cheeks growing hot, looking like Alice when she has fallen through the rabbit hole and arrived in a whole new world. It's crazy.

Eventually my patience runs out. It is our duty lunchtime in the school shop and Reece leans on the counter for ages, nattering to Ellen about nothing. Customers come and go. We sell out of penny sweets and apples and he's still stuck there. Then, when we are putting the stock away, I hiss to her: 'Get rid of him, Ell, for goodness' sake. He's doing my head in standing around like a lovesick calf. Why doesn't he go and get himself a life?'

'He's going for lunch now and so are we . . .' Ellen mutters.

'You must be joking! I am not going into late lunch with a great spoony Year Eight with jug ears and zits,' I say viciously. 'If you want to go with him you go on your own.'

'Oh, Rosie!' Ellen's eyes are suspiciously bright. 'You don't mean that.'

'It's him or me,' I say. 'It's make-your-mind-up-time.'

It's me. I knew it would be. Ellen is just too soft for her own good. Heaven knows what would happen to her if she didn't have me to look after her.

Things are pretty grim at home too. The two cousins are like elderly invalids rather than children. They both stay in bed all day rising at about three or four in the afternoon, taking a bath, and then sitting in front of the television with the curtains drawn until supper time. Mum has had Crystal down to the doctor in case she is ailing too. The doc said Crystal might be a bit anaemic or very over-tired and homesick and just to let her do things at her own pace for a few days. He also gave her a tonic to buck her up.

Mum doesn't seem to mind them staying in bed. 'At least I know where they are and what they are doing. And it means I can get on with my marking and writing,' she says with a patient smile. But I think it's really weird and depressing. I hate running upstairs with trays of drinks and food and medicine for them. And it's awful having them drooping about in their pyjamas and sitting with blankets over their knees. It's like living in a sanatorium for grumpy little girls. There's never a smile or a thank-you from either of them.

On the last day of term Ash says, 'When am I going to meet these cousins of yours?'

'Big thrill for you—I don't think,' I mutter. 'Come and see them if you want.'

'You are too kind,' he mocks.

Mum is working in her study. 'Would you like a cup of tea? Ash is here. I'm going to make us some coffee,' I say to her. Since my brainwave about the arranged marriage between Mum and Ralph I've been more open about my friendship with Ash. I have this lovely dream that when they tie the knot they will say to people, 'It's so perfect—our teenagers are friends too.' And my, what a happy family we will be!

'Some tea would be lovely. Thank you,' Mum says. 'Ask the girls if they'd like some hot chocolate, would you please, darling. I'm trying to build them up.' Mum looks up from her manuscript and smiles. 'I made some flapjack for them too. Hamish and I were talking about how good oats are for you.'

'Yes, of course,' I say through gritted teeth. 'Oats! What a good idea. Why didn't we think about it before? They'll soon be racing around like little racehorses, won't they?'

I go into the kitchen shaking my head. Honestly, I don't understand Hamish MacCrimmon. He is professor of poetry at one of the most prestigious universities in the country, yet he's always talking about daft things like oats and drains and boilers. He really ought to concentrate on stanzas and haiku and world issues or he'll be getting the push. I am sure that most of the undergraduates must be more intellectually stimulating than him.

When I take Mum her mug of tea she asks, 'When do your rehearsals start?'

'Next week—but we are being measured for costumes tomorrow. Do you think the invalids will be well enough to come with me? And can I have a deposit, please, for their costumes?'

Mum looks anxious. 'Oh, dear, how much will that be?'

'Quite a bit—it mounts up when there are two. And Mrs Valente said she'd give them walk-on parts in lots of the numbers—because rehearsals can be deadly boring if you don't have enough to do. Milo did leave a cheque or some money for them, didn't he?' I ask Mum suspiciously.

'Well, he couldn't find his cheque book while he was here—you know how disorganized he is. And he did promise he would post it from the airport. But I'm afraid it hasn't arrived, so I suppose he was in too much of a rush and forgot about it.' Looking at my worried face she adds reassuringly, 'But I'm sure he'll have sent it off as soon as he got to the States and remembered. I just don't know how long it will take to arrive. But don't worry. I'll manage.'

'Do you have an address for him?'

'No . . . But he said he would write when he was settled. He's sure to phone soon. I'm sure that he'll want to speak to the girls,' she says brightly.

'Yes, of course,' I say, shutting the door quietly. Mum is so trusting and kind. (Or is she naive and easily duped? a miserable little voice in my head asks.) That is why she needs someone like Ralph. No one would pull the wool over his eyes. Not likely!

Ash is sitting at the kitchen table waiting for me. He has managed to make some half-decent toast on our ancient grill which is quite an achievement. 'Well, where are they—these cousins of yours? I thought they'd be rushing around and making a noise,' he says.

'Fat chance—they are the original sloth children. Goodness knows how they will cope with rehearsals and shows—if I ever manage to get them there. After we've had our toast we'll go into the sickroom and say hello to them. But don't make any loud noises or sudden movements—they're a bit fragile.'

'HI!' I say loudly, marching into the sitting room with a tray of food and drink. 'Wakey, wakey, rise and shine—there's a friend of mine here to see you. Ash, this is Crystal and Cara. C and C, this is Ash from next door.'

I put the tray down and open the curtains with a flourish. As the afternoon sunlight streams in the dim dancing picture on our ancient television set disappears. 'And how are we today?' I ask.

Crystal looks terrible. Her hair hangs in greasy curtains and her face is so pale it is almost green. Worst of all she is wearing kiddies' brushed cotton pyjamas with toast crumbs and tea stains down the front. She looks gross, and she obviously knows it because she tries to hide herself under the tartan blanket draped over her knees. Ash's eyes widen with astonishment as he stares at her. In contrast Cara is curled up like a kitten under a patchwork quilt and she looks sleepy and rather sweet.

'Hello, nice to meet you both,' Ash says. He is backing out of the room rather hurriedly, looking a bit shaken.

'Do they sit there all day like that?' he asks, when we are alone in the kitchen.

'Yes, it's awful, isn't it? Cara at least has been ill, but Crystal just can't be bothered to get up.'

'Do you think she's suffering from depression?' he asks concerned.

'I don't know. But I will be after a whole summer holiday with them.'

Ash laughs. 'No you won't. Nothing ever gets you down.'

'Yes, it does,' I say, a bit stung by this casual dismissal of my plight.

'Like what?' Ash says, grinning.

'Like not having enough money and this house being such a tip and not going on holiday and Jessica's horrid party and my little cousins being foul and . . .' I stop because I feel quite tearful. And I haven't even got started on my lack of boobs and the loneliness of my life without Joshua as a romantic hero. There are some things you can't possibly tell a boy—even if he is one of your very best friends.

'And I get depressed about not having a father . . .' I burst out suddenly. This takes me by surprise because I'd always thought I didn't mind not having a dad—working along the lines that what you've never had you never miss. But now I know I do mind. I mind very much. And I know then, in a painful moment of truth, that I want to arrange this marriage between Ralph and my mum not just for them but also for me and Ash. Because I need a dad and I suspect he might need a mum (or he wouldn't want a scarf or a jumper to cuddle). It's as simple as that.

'Shit . . .' Ash mutters, frowning. 'I'm sorry. What I meant was you don't get upset about silly little things—the way Ellen does. She's been in a real moody since that bloody party.'

He comes over and stands by my shoulder, and then he pats my back rather awkwardly, as if I am a baby who needs burping. 'Rosie . . .' he says, and then there is a long awkward silence between us. I am unable to speak because I can feel tears prickling the back of my eyes and my chin starting to wobble and I know if I say a word I will blub.

'Rosie . . .' he starts again. 'Me and Dad are going across to the cottage on Sunday for a week—it's rather primitive. You know how Dad likes that kind of thing—getting back to nature and crap like that. And we sail every day on the lake even if it's pissing it down. But you could wear a life jacket and there's a little spare bedroom at the back. You could . . . I mean—if you thought it wouldn't be too boring—you could come with us.' He gives my back another quick rub and then steps back. He isn't looking at me. He is frowning into the distance. I feel a wave of gratitude and affection rising up inside me—driving the tears away and making me feel better.

'That is so kind of you, Ash. But I am meant to be looking after the cousins . . .' I say wistfully.

'They don't seem to need much looking after. They are more like pot plants than kids. You could ask your mother. I mean if you'd like to come.'

'Oh, Ash. I'd love to come. It would be brilliant. But what about your dad?'

'He did ask me if I wanted to invite a friend along but there's no one at school I wanted to go with . . . apart from you,' he adds quickly.

'I'll ask my mother,' I say. 'Thanks, Ash.' I think about how popular he is at school. There are loads of people he could have invited and who would have been only too pleased to go with him.

'Talk to your mum. I'll ring you later,' he says.

I go to find Mum but she is rushing off to catch the post. 'Hamish is in Scotland and I promised I'd get these to him by tomorrow. Speak to you when I get back,' she says, kissing my face quickly.

'What are they?' I ask, rather grumpily.

'My new poems,' she says shyly. 'I do value his opinion. Working on your own can be very lonely.'

'You can always show them to me,' I say.

'I know I can, darling, and I do appreciate your opinion,' she says gratefully. But she still dashes off to the postbox. I sigh and feel irritable because I am desperate to talk to her about going away with Ash and Ralph. I am really excited about it. Not that sailing grabs me one bit. But it will be great to spend a week with Ash. And I am also thinking of all the opportunities I will have to drop complimentary things about Mum into the conversation when Ralph is around. By the time I have finished Ralph will know she is a woman made in heaven especially for him.

I am standing doing the washing up, lost in a lovely daydream about my week in the Lake District, when I am abruptly brought down to earth by Crystal's voice.

'Does that boy live over there?'

I had been so caught up in my fantasy world that I hadn't even realized she was in the kitchen with me. She is over by the window and has pulled up a corner of the calico blind so that she can peek through and see the coach house.

For a moment I just gawp at her. She has washed her hair and fluffed it up with a hairdryer so it is a great swirling mass of stripy darkness. She is wearing a tiny denim skirt and a top with a huge neckline so her shoulders are on show. To complete the clubbing look she is also wearing high heels. When she turns to face me I see her mouth is red, and her lashes darkened so her eyes look as if they have been put in place with a sooty finger. She looks amazing and about sixteen. I swallow hard.

'Are you going out?' I ask rather nervously.

She places a hand on her hip and gives me a disgusted look. 'Well—there's nothing to stay in for—is there? Does that boy live over there?' she asks again.

'Yes,' I mutter.

'What did you say he's called?'

'Ash—Ashley.'

'That's nice,' she says, smiling. 'Is he your boyfriend?'

Just for a second I am tempted to say 'Yes'. I don't know why I want to tell such a lie, but I do, and my face heats.

'No . . . just a mate . . .' I mutter miserably.

'I see,' she says dismissively. Then she turns her back on me and goes back to peering through the chink in the blind.

'Please don't do that,' I say a bit snappily. It's making me feel really miserable watching her. I am reminded painfully of doing something similar when I peeped through the pink pane on the stairs. I argue to myself that it's different when you are friends, you can do things like that, and anyway I've confessed to Ash about it. And that makes it better. But it doesn't take away the nasty feeling I've got.

'My mother put that up for privacy. It's very important with our two homes being so close,' I say a bit pompously. 'Please don't pull it up. We can't afford frosted glass and my mother will be upset if the blind is ruined.'

'Oh shut up. It's not a blind. It's a dirty old bit of material,' Crystal says.

'It doesn't matter what the hell it is. It's all we've got— so leave it alone!' I move around her and pull the calico back over the window. The drawing pin that held it in place is on the floor. I pick it up and make a great play of pushing it back in.

'It's not even nailed . . .' Crystal says.

'Yes, well, if your father pays up the money he is meant to be sending for your keep maybe we will be able to afford a proper blind.'

I regret the words as soon as I have said them. It's a really snide comment and I know I shouldn't have said it. She is after all only eleven and a guest in my home. But she has rattled me. I resent the fact that until Milo pays up we will have even less money than usual, which is bad news, especially with the boiler being so temperamental and the roof leaking. Also I have asked Mrs Valente a huge favour to get them parts in the show— we don't even know if they can dance at all. But when I explained the position to Mrs Valente she was really kind and said she would find them something to do. 'We can always have an extra flower girl or two. All they'll have to do is walk on stage and smile,' she said kindly.

I thought that I had organized it so well. It was all set up to be so much fun. Having them to stay, taking them along to rehearsals and us being in the show together. There was also the hope that they would create a family atmosphere which would help Mum and Ralph bond as a couple.

Crystal is eyeing me with a look that would freeze the sea. I eye her back.

'What money is this you're talking about?' she asks aggressively.

'Your father is meant to be paying for your keep,' I say coolly.

'We're guests, Auntie Hal asked us to stay. She wanted us here . . .' Crystal doesn't sound so sure of herself now and I try to soften my tone as I reply.

'He asked her to take you both and offered to pay. My mother has a great deal of trouble keeping this house going on her salary. There are loads of things that need doing to it. We don't have any spare money.'

'But Auntie Hal wanted us to come . . . she said so,' Crystal says, her voice suddenly a bit shrill and scared. And just for a second the façade of a hard-faced grown-up slips and I see anxiety in her expression. For one of the few times since she arrived, apart from when she was sleeping, she looks like a child—a scared child who might cry at any moment. I feel terrible.

'Well, of course she wanted you to come to stay. We both did,' I say brusquely. 'And when the cheque arrives it will be fine. It's just I need to pay for your costumes in the show.'

'There won't be a cheque. Milo hasn't even got a bank account. He's a bankrupt.' She says it coolly. The mask is back—she says it as if she couldn't care less. 'And I don't want to be in your stupid dance show anyway. So I won't need a costume or anything like that. I hate dancing . . .' Having dropped that little bombshell she minces across the kitchen in her high heels. 'I'm going to take Cara out for a walk. Auntie Hal says we can go and get an ice cream.'

'It's a long walk to the shops,' I say.

'The exercise will be good for us,' she says smugly.

There's nothing I can do. Mum comes into the kitchen and rummages in the teapot for some money. And then I am dispatched with them to walk down to the shops to buy ice cream. I feel like an unexploded bomb and have to do deep breathing to calm myself down.

Everything is going wrong. And I know that I can't possibly ask Mum if I can go to the Lake District with Ash and Ralph now. For a start I'd need to take spending money with me, money we haven't got. (And aren't likely to get if what Crystal said about Milo is true.) Also I'd need loads of new gear like a decent waterproof for sailing and spare pair of trainers—and there is no way we could manage that.

I have a tiny bit of Christmas and birthday money left in my post office account but I'll need that over the summer—especially as I have given up any hope of my gorgeous embroidered jeans ever fitting me again. Aside from money the other big problem is Crystal and Cara. There's no way they can be left to wander the streets while Mum is trying to read dissertations and write magical poems. Cara is only just four and Crystal looks like a girl with big ideas who is looking for trouble. They are going to need constant watching. Why couldn't they have stayed as the pot-plant children in their pyjamas? Oh-my-goodness-can-this-whole-situation-get-any-worse?

7

Crystal is obviously disappointed that we don't see Ash (or any other boys) on our long trail down to the shops. She mutters about how boring everything is. I suppose a small Northern city with ancient walls, a cathedral, and a university must seem like a graveyard after London.

We buy ice cream and trudge back up the hill to home. It's not a particularly warm day. The sun disappears completely while we are out and Crystal's legs become goosefleshy. 'The weather is so horrible here,' she complains. 'Is it always cold like this?' she adds querulously.

'Yes, apart from when we have a heatwave,' I say smugly. I don't care if she does hate it here. I hate having her to stay. And I particularly hate the fact that my mother gave me a hard-earned five pound note to buy ice cream and they both decided they wanted a Magnum so there's not much change left. I should have insisted they had lollies but I was too shell-shocked by their cheek and lack of manners to start arguing with them in front of a shop full of people. I am seething inside, especially as I haven't bought anything for myself. This was a silent protest about their rudeness which I'm starting to regret.

'Would you like a bite of mine?' Cara offers.

'No thanks,' I say abruptly, looking away quickly, even though I'd love a bite. I had just been thinking how scrummy it looked.

When we were in the shop I couldn't buy myself anything with that fiver because it seemed to symbolize my lost holiday with Ash. As I handed it over and pocketed the small change it was like the end of all my hopes. Just thinking about how much fun Ash and I could have had in the Lake District (even if we did have to go sailing every day) makes me feel like crying. And I know that I daren't even mention it to Mum and unburden some of my misery.

For a start I'm not sure if I can control myself if I begin talking about Crystal and Cara. I fear I could end up having a tantrum or at the very least a major moan about how awful they are. I particularly don't want to make Mum miserable when she's busy writing. Unhappiness gives her writer's block and that's the last thing we need at the moment. Also I'd hate her to know how unhappy I am about not going away on holiday. I know for a fact that it would make her feel guilty because she's always tried really hard to make sure I didn't miss out on things just because she is a single parent.

But it's not just all those things which stop my tongue—I am also painfully aware that my cousins coming to stay and joining in the dance show was my bright idea. Why on earth didn't I think of some other way to get Mum and Ralph together? If I hadn't offered to look after them Mum would have said 'No' to Milo. Crystal and Cara are here because of me. It is completely my fault. I should have kept my big mouth shut.

Knowing all this makes me feel terrible. I am desperate to see Ash because if I don't talk to someone about it all I shall go crazy.

'I'm looking forward to going to dancing,' Cara says shyly. She has been walking along holding my hand, while Crystal trails behind us. 'I used to dance with Mummy. Mummy is a ballerina. She's dancing on ships now. She sends us lovely postcards.'

'Does she?' I say, as if I hadn't noticed. In fact sometimes as many as three postcards will arrive together in the mail for them. Their mother seems to write one every day although she can't always send them. She is sailing round the Med. I feel really sorry for Cara. I wonder how I would have managed without my mum when I was four. I squeeze her hand and say, 'Tomorrow we have to go and be measured for our costumes.' I tell her all about the numbers we are doing in the show and she gets quite excited.

'Crystal, Crystal,' she says hopping about. 'I'm going to be a flower fairy and a raindrop and a baby piglet. I'll like to be a piglet best of all. Can I snort?'

She starts to make piggy grunts which make me smile. Now she's up and about and clean she's quite fun. But Crystal just scowls and ignores us.

'Next week we start rehearsals. We have to go to the studio every day and learn all the dances,' I tell her. 'You'll have to help me because I'm a chaperone and I look after all the little ones and make sure they are ready when they are needed.'

'Will I get to wear my piggy costume?' Cara asks delightedly.

'No, of course not,' I say. 'You won't wear your costumes until the dress rehearsal. You will have to wear your practice clothes for rehearsals: leotard and tights and a little skirt for when you are a flower fairy. You know the kind of thing . . .'

She obviously doesn't know. She is looking puzzled.

'You do have practice clothes for dancing, don't you?' I ask Crystal.

'No,' she says abruptly.

'You must have practice clothes,' I say to Cara, trying to stem my rising feeling of panic. 'When you danced with your mummy what did you wear?'

'Oh, we dressed up,' Cara says happily. 'Mummy made me a skirt from scarves and a princess party dress from a beautiful petticoat.'

'But have you got some ballet shoes?' I ask anxiously.

'Mummy has ballet shoes, lots of them, tappy ones

and ones for standing on her toes. They are lovely.'

'What did you wear when you danced with Mummy?'

'My bare wiggly tiggly toes,' Cara says, laughing.

I stop abruptly and turn to Crystal.

'You must have practice clothes and shoes from when you were little. I'm going to need some things for Cara. Where are the ones that you used? Didn't Mum tell you to bring them?'

Crystal shrugs. 'They got left behind somewhere . . .' she mutters. 'We don't have anything like that. So you can forget all about being in stupid dance shows,' she adds nastily to Cara.

'Surely you still have something, anything?' I say pleadingly to Crystal. 'Some ballet shoes or tights; you had the lot when you wore that lovely cygnet costume—anything will do. I can swap them in the seconds shop, you see. But things like that new cost such a lot of money.'

'Look, we had to do a moonlight from a flat because we couldn't pay the rent and everything got left behind.' Crystal's voice is an ugly whisper. 'We lost our toys, our clothes, Cara's buggy, even the bleeding cat. So no—we don't have any stupid, frigging leotards or tights or stupid tutus.' She leans over Cara and adds viciously, 'Now—will you shut up whingeing about dancing—you stupid eejit!'

I stare at her for a long moment feeling sick. A moonlight sounds awful; going off without paying, leaving all your stuff behind; it is incomprehensible to me.

Cara is looking confused, tearful even, and her Magnum is starting to drip down her chin and fingers. 'Can I still be a piggy? I want to be a dancing pig . . .' she says to me in a wavering whisper.

'Yes, of course you can be a piggy and all the rest of the parts as well. Take no notice of your sister—she's a bitch.' I automatically take a tissue from my pocket and mop her face and hands. 'Eat up your ice cream. I'll find you some practice clothes to wear. We have a great seconds shop at the Academy. Don't worry. I'll get you a lovely pair of pink tights and a white leotard and woolly crossover and a little net skirt—you'll need that because the flower fairies have to hold their skirts when they gallop. Can you gallop?' I am talking fast to take our minds off what Crystal has said.

'Yes, yes,' Cara says. 'I can gallop and skip and point my toe and I can curtsy.'

'I bet you'll be one of the best in the class,' I say to cheer her up.

'Can we do dancing when we get home?' Cara asks. 'I want to show you and Auntie Hal my dancing!' Her small hand in mine is warm and sticky and I give her fingers another little squeeze. Poor little kid—fancy having Crystal for a sister on top of everything else.

'Yes, of course we'll do dancing,' I say kindly. 'But finish your ice cream up before it melts.'

Worrying about Cara's practice clothes and lack of money takes my mind off my other problems. I had been quite upset at the thought of telling Ash I couldn't go with him to the Lakes. But when I tell him he seems strangely relieved. I am hurt until he explains.

'Dad has bought a tent. He wants us to have a couple of nights in a bivvy,' he explains.

'Bivvy?' I echo.

'Bivouac. Living rough. I was worried about you. No loos or anything . . .' Ash grins at me. 'Cooking on a campfire, that sort of thing. A kind of survival course.'

'Oh-my-goodness-how-absolutely-awful!' I exclaim. 'Do you have to catch your own food as well?'

'No . . .' Ash says, but he doesn't sound very certain about this. 'Unless we do some fishing, I suppose we could eat those.'

'Or you could try roast hedgehog and dandelions . . .' I suggest.

'Or rabbit stew with wild carrots,' Ash adds.

71

'We don't get wild carrots in this country,' I say.

'I'm sure we do. Anyway dandelion roots would be fine. You can make coffee out of them. I expect they'd be delicious pan-fried in some butter,' he says with a grin.

'Great,' I say. 'I should take a secret supply of chocolate and Kendal mint cake if I were you. That's probably why they make Kendal mint cake up there—a special food for barmy people who want go off and live wild in the hills.'

'It *is* a bit of a bonkers idea,' Ash admits. 'But Dad . . .' He stops and then adds very quietly, 'I'd much rather have stayed in the cottage with you. But Dad was really weird about it.'

'Doesn't he like me?' I ask, suddenly hurt and ready to be really upset. If Ralph doesn't like me that could be a real problem when he marries my mother. And I do so want them to get married and for us all to live happily ever after.

'Of course he likes you. He likes you loads. He's always saying what a live wire you are and good stuff like that . . .' Ash shrugs and then says, 'It's just when I asked if you could come with us he suddenly got all preachy and started on about meaningful relationships and sex and respecting women. Then he got all technical about teenage pregnancy and STIs and crap like that. God! Don't parents drive you insane sometimes! I kept on telling him it was way too much information but he wouldn't shut up.'

I can't look at Ash. I can feel a dreadful hotness spreading up over my neck and face. It's awful to think of Ralph giving him a huge lecture about sex because of me. It makes me feel really spooked. What on earth did Ralph think we were going to be doing in the Lake District? This is worse than school when everyone thinks as soon as you talk to a boy you want to be snogging him.

'Do you want to go bivvying?' I ask, in a desperate attempt to change the subject.

'No, not really. I don't even like sailing very much, not that I'd ever tell Dad that. I was hoping if you came to the cottage we might do something else for a change,' Ash admits.

'Can't you suggest it, or get him to go somewhere else?'

'It would only be another activity holiday. He can't seem to get his head around anything else. One year we did painting and pottery in Cornwall. That was the absolute pits. It was full of creepy old women who fawned over Dad and treated me like a pet dog.'

'I suppose sitting on a beach or hanging out in cafés isn't really your dad's scene. He's so energetic.'

'He's not really a holiday person . . . He and my mother were mad keen on sailing. That's how they met. They spent all their spare time on their boat until I arrived. It's a shame he can't meet someone—someone who likes sailing . . .' Ash says.

I try to sound nonchalant as I ask, 'Do you mean a woman?'

'Well—yes . . . of course,' Ash says.

'To go sailing with?' I ask innocently.

'Yes—and to marry. When he was giving me all this grief about relationships and the female perspective I suddenly realized how shit it must be for him on his own . . . He started talking about my mother and how they met and how much he respected her and I thought at one point that he was going to cry.'

'Oh, that's terrible . . .' I say. I am really shocked and upset. I have never thought of Ralph being lonely. He is always so focused, moving at a pace that makes everyone else look slow. 'But he always seems so busy and happy,' I add.

'I think he just rushes around all the time to hide the pain of losing her,' Ash says quietly. 'That's why I agreed to the bivvy. I expect by the time we've finished we'll be too wet, cold, and exhausted to think about anything else. That's generally how I feel after a day sailing.'

'Well, I'm going to be stuck here with the cousins from hell . . .' I say, and then I have a really good moan about them. (Although I miss out Crystal's spying and unhealthy interest in him because he would be totally grossed out by it.)

Ash is great—he listens until I have told him everything. 'Do you think I should tell my mother there is no chance of a cheque from Milo?' I ask him.

'No. You don't want to worry her if there is no need. After all, he might get a banker's draft or get a friend to write a cheque for him. I expect it will all turn out OK. He's obviously going to be in the money if he's in the States making a CD. He's bound to send some cash eventually. Why don't you tell Mrs Valente you'll pay later and stop worrying? Milo's money will arrive and you can tell your mother then what is owing.'

'She's busy working on a new book of poems; the other sold rather well. She's been asked to go to the Ilkley Literature Festival in the autumn and read some of them,' I say quickly. I don't want him to think my mother is flaky and can't cope with life. 'She needs peace and quiet and not to be worried when she's writing. It's like going into a different world and she doesn't need any emotional luggage from this one to hold her back.'

'Sounds a bit like living in a bivvy,' he said. 'A minimalist lifestyle.'

'But with a bathroom,' I say and we both laugh.

'Yes, you're right, that's what I'll do,' I say gratefully. I am so lucky to have him for a friend. He's so sensible. I feel loads better.

I am also very cheered that he wants his dad to get married. We all seem to be thinking along the same lines, which is great. I have a real battle to stop myself from telling him my plan for our parents. Cara comes to find me and breaks up our conversation and it's just as well because I am on the verge of telling him all about it. It's a miracle that I haven't blurted everything by now. I am quite proud of myself because Ash always used to say I was a blabbermouth and couldn't keep secrets; obviously this isn't true any more. I really feel that maturity and good judgement and discretion are the sort of words that should be used to describe me these days. I hug the secret to myself. I think about the fun and laughs Ash and I will have when Ralph and my mother finally get married and I tell him how I planned it all.

8

Taking Crystal and Cara to the Valente Academy is traumatic. Crystal is in a major sulk. She also gets herself dressed up as if she is going to a party. Part of me is irritated because she looks fantastic, like a dark-eyed porcelain doll, and part of me is shocked again that she can make herself look so grown-up. I'm pretty sure that her bust is at least two sizes bigger than mine which makes me feel terrible. I've never minded being so skinny and boyish before, but now it seems like a curse when even eleven year olds can look more mature than me.

Cara is really excited about going to be measured for her costumes and spends the whole time talking and giggling. She's very sweet, but her exuberance throws Crystal's sulking into sharp relief. When Crystal is in the room it's like having a thundercloud hanging over us. The very air seems thick with her mood. And I am conscious every time I speak that she is listening and thinking how stupid I am. She has gone to great pains to tell me that dancing, all dancing, but especially ballet, is the pits and an absolute waste of time. She also makes horrible remarks to Cara about how silly it all is. Cara doesn't seem to take any notice but it gets on my nerves.

From pumping Cara I know that Crystal used to take dancing lessons and I wonder if she was very bad at it and that's why she is so negative. Lots of people are forced into doing things like dancing and piano lessons because their mothers want them to. And you can always tell which ones they are in a class. I bet Crystal's teacher was relieved when she didn't have to look at Crystal's sulky face any more. She is a most disagreeable girl.

Our costume call is at ten but I want to get to the Academy early so that Mrs Valente and I can discuss the rehearsals. I help her organize the rota and sort out who is going to chaperone the little ones. I'd warned Crystal and Cara what time we would have to leave and Cara rocketed out of bed and has been really helpful. But Crystal has moved the whole time in slow motion so I end up trying to hurry them through town. The narrow streets are already busy and Crystal seems to use this as an excuse to walk as if she is Mary Queen of Scots going to have her head chopped off.

By the time we arrive I feel really stressed. Despite Ash's optimism and cheering words I am still anxious about money for costumes and practice clothes. I had hoped right up until we left home that something might arrive from Milo in the post, or Mum might remember and give me a cheque. But she is lost in a world of poetry at the moment; it makes her extra forgetful, and I don't want to worry her.

I learnt early on in life that if I wanted things for school like cookery ingredients and PE kit I would have to organize them myself. And I always sort out my own dancing clothes. Mum once put all my leotards and tights in the wash with some dusters she'd used for cleaning the brass. (Auntie May left us a huge collection of warming pans and kettles and every so often Mum is riddled with guilt at the state of them and spends a day polishing.) The pong from my clothes after the Brasso wash was utterly vile. No one would stand next to me at the barre—it was total humiliation—and during the class the hotter and sweatier I got the stronger the smell became. Ash said it was an interesting chemical reaction between the Brasso trapped in the fabric and my perspiration but I was too hacked off to care about a scientific explanation. I was pig sick of all the jokes about

'A Rose by any other name . . .' and stuff like that.

Remembering all this makes me feel doubly depressed. I just have to hope when Mum and Ralph are married she will get to be a bit more organized. It's terrible not having a cheque because one of my jobs at the start of rehearsals is to make a list of who has paid. It seems really dreadful to be one of the non-payers. I've always really despised the parents who drop their little ones off for this first rehearsal call without coming in or leaving money for a deposit. And now here I am—doing the same thing. But I have decided that I will be upfront with Mrs Valente about it—embarrassing though it is. It is, after all, Milo's fault we haven't got the money—not mine or Mum's—but I still feel implicated—as if Milo's lack of integrity somehow rubs off on us.

Ash is lucky in more ways than one to have that bank-manager uncle. He's got good genes on his side. Whereas I've got a big question mark over my father—Mum is struck dumb every time I try to get the conversation around to him. And to cap it all I have a black sheep of an uncle who has landed me with the cousin from hell.

I've drawn out all the money from my post office book. I want to buy Ash a 'going-on-holiday present', and keep myself in pocket money for a couple of weeks so I don't have to ask Mum for anything. It must be costing her a fortune to keep Crystal and Cara; we are having to buy loads more food, and have the heating on in the evenings unless the weather is boiling hot. They are like a couple of sensitive plants which need to be kept at greenhouse temperature.

Mrs Valente is great with Crystal. She offers her a whole choice of jobs to do. Crystal just looks sullen when she is asked if she'd like to help with lighting, sound, or stage management. 'Or you can have some parts in the show. That would be more fun, wouldn't it?' Mrs Valente says cheerfully. 'At least you'll have some pretty costumes and something to keep you busy. Rose is here from dawn to dusk once we start rehearsing.' Mrs Valente gives Crystal a long appraising look. 'We are going to be doing a wonderful can-can number—it will be such fun. The dance is very free and easy—you just need lots of enthusiasm. You could keep up on the back row, I expect. Have you done much dancing before, dear?' she asks.

'Did my grades . . .' Crystal mumbles after a long pause—Mrs Valente is not someone who you ignore or refuse to answer however much you want to.

'Well, you could be on the front line with those lovely long legs. I am going to need a lead can-can girl and you might be just the right person.'

'All right . . .' Crystal mutters, although she doesn't sound very confident.

'You'll soon find your feet.' Mrs Valente laughs at her own pun. 'Especially with Rose to help you—she's an old timer. She's been in every show for the last ten years. And this year she is top of the bill again.' Mrs Valente turns to me and smiles. 'I've worked out a wonderful pas de deux for you and Amelia. *Beauty and the Beast*—it will be sensational.'

'Will I be the Beast?' I ask excitedly. Mrs Valente took us to Newcastle to see the Northern Ballet Company dance *Beauty and the Beast* last year—and I was knocked out by the part of the Beast. He gets to do some great solos, especially when he's angry. He throws himself against the walls and really makes you feel his pain.

Mrs Valente smiles at me a bit sympathetically. 'I'm afraid Amelia will have to take the part of the Beast. She's shot up this year and is quite a lot taller than you. But you will make a lovely Beauty. It's a tender role. It will challenge you,' she adds reassuringly.

'Yes, of course. I shall love it,' I say brightly, swallowing down my disappointment. It seems that everyone is taller, and bustier, than me. I shall be getting a complex if I don't start growing soon.

'Shall we start measuring?' Mrs Valente says looking down at Cara's excited face.

'I will get to be a piggy, won't I?' Cara asks.

'Oh, yes,' Mrs Valente says. 'We are doing some scenes from *Animal Farm*. The pigs are very important. Do you like singing? We will need some piggy voices.'

'Oh, I love singing. Mummy used to sing all the time with us.'

If Mrs Valente sees Crystal reach over and pinch Cara's arm she ignores it. So do I. Cara tries not to cry and blinks back tears. Mrs Valente takes the measurements, talking soothingly as she does so of what the costumes will look like. It cheers Cara up no end. She volunteers to do everything. Oh yes, she would like to be a puppet, a robin, a raindrop, and a flower fairy, and of course a pig. Although it's a relief to have someone smiling and being enthusiastic, I am doing rapid sums in my head and trying to work out how much it is all going to cost.

Because I spend all day Saturday helping Mrs Valente with the younger children I get my costumes free. 'A perk of the job,' Mrs Valente always says. And it's been great. But I know that sometimes I have been staggered at how much it costs if you have two or even three little girls in one family. Mrs Waugh spends a fortune which is probably why she has to house-sit for the Brownes.

'There we are—that's splendid,' Mrs Valente says with satisfaction, when all our measurements have been taken and a list has been made of the numbers we will be in. Crystal has ended up with four numbers—nothing difficult—just the can-can, a bit of modern, and two walk-on parts—but even so she is looking shell-shocked. She has discovered, like the rest of us, that saying 'No' to Mrs Valente when she's being enthusiastic is impossible.

Mrs Valente looks at my face and says, 'That's what you wanted, isn't it, Rose, dear? These parts will keep you all busy. The girls won't be hanging around waiting for you.'

'Oh yes,' I say gratefully. 'It's so very kind of you. I do . . . we do appreciate it,' I add quickly. I asked her for a favour. I can't be miffed now that she's done it for me. I wasn't to know when I asked that bloody Milo is a bankrupt. 'It's just I need to get some practice clothes for them from the swap shop. And I don't have a cheque this week . . .' I look down at the bill in my hand and try not to groan at the total. 'I will bring it soon,' I add, as I bite at my lip, feeling humiliated.

'That is absolutely fine,' Mrs Valente says reassuringly. 'Just bring it when you can. I'm glad to be able to help. Just take what you need from the swap shop and put it down in the book.'

The first group of babies starts to arrive to be measured up and I don't have a chance to thank her properly. I get the payment book out and start a new page wishing I could put my name at the top with 'paid' next to it. The amount for the costumes is staggeringly high and I haven't got their practice clothes yet. They both need ballet, tap, and character shoes. It will run into hundreds by the time we've finished. I shall have to start praying hard that Ash is right and Milo's money arrives soon.

On the way home, when Cara finally shuts up about her robin costume, which has taken over from pig as favourite of the day, I turn to Crystal and say, 'There, that wasn't too bad, was it?' in what I hope is a conciliatory tone. I don't think I can face the rest of the holidays if she is going to be this moody. Now she's agreed to join in with the dancing I think we should be friends. Well, if not friends—at least a little bit friendly. Especially as I have run up a huge debt in the swap shop to get them kitted out with practice clothes. 'At least Mrs Valente didn't make you join in the ballet numbers,' I say kindly. 'The Pre-Elementary group is doing a corps de ballet adaptation from *Blue Train* and it's really difficult. They've been learning it since Easter but they are going to sweat to get it polished and ready in two weeks.'

'Crystal loves ballet . . .' Cara says in a whisper to me.

Crystal yells, 'Shut up, eejit!' And she reaches over and pulls at Cara's hair with a vicious yank that makes Cara cry out in pain.

I shout furiously, 'Stop that, you little bitch. Leave her alone. Why did you do that?'

'I hate frigging ballet. And I hate you both! And I don't want to be in your horrible dance show!' Crystal cries angrily. 'I hope it's a real flop and no one comes to see it and . . .'

'Oh, for heaven's sake—grow up!' I scream. 'No one is making you do ballet. And a scarecrow with a wooden leg could keep up with the modern and can-can number Mrs Valente has put you in. And don't even start to scheme about botching it up and spoiling things for everyone else. Because no one will be watching you or caring what you are doing in the show, you stupid nasty little girl. Parents come along to watch their own precious darlings. You can fall flat on your face and die and no one will even notice. So just carry on being grotty and bad-tempered and suit yourself! Go ahead and make a complete arse of yourself—no one cares!'

There's a silence while I get my breath. They are both staring at me round-eyed with astonishment. It's the first time I've lost my temper with them. It's obviously given them a bit of a jolt.

Cara pulls at my hand; her eyes are brimming. 'But Auntie Hal will be watching me when I am a piggy and a robin, won't she? I won't fall on my bum and no one will care?' she asks.

I suddenly realize how tactless my outburst was—and not strictly true—because Mrs Valente will go ape if Crystal starts to muck about. Any larking from anyone and they're out of the show and Mrs Valente doesn't care if the costumes are made and parents have paid. It's a huge undertaking to get a show like ours rehearsed and staged in such a short space of time and she expects high standards—even from the babies. No talking or giggling when others are performing—being ready for your cues—learning your steps and words—being polite and punctual. As one of the chaperones it's my job to make sure that everyone is behaving properly. I feel sick at the thought of the harm Crystal could do if she starts answering me back and being gobby. I must make sure she isn't in any of my groups.

'Of course Auntie Hal will watch you,' I say a bit desperately to Cara. 'And I'll watch you too. Don't cry . . .' I suddenly have a brilliant idea. 'And my friend Ellen has a video recorder. I'll ask her if she will come to the dress rehearsal to film the bits you are in. And then you can send it to your daddy and mummy and they can see you. Then you'll be a movie star as well as a robin and a piggy.'

'Will she film Crystal too?' Cara asks.

'Oh dear no. It might break the camera filming Crystal's ugly mug! We'll just make a video of you,' I whisper. Crystal is trailing miles behind and I am confident she can't hear us.

Cara giggles and whispers, 'Goody . . .'

All this nastiness makes me feel really depressed. I am longing to see Ash. I patrol the skylight and the kitchen for the rest of the day but there is no sign of him.

I get up very early in the morning because I am scared I might miss him. Thankfully today I am in luck. The rose-tinted pane shows me him and Ralph packing the car with their tent, rucksacks, and neat boxes of provisions.

I wander out into the yard as if I am always up and dressed by seven thirty on a Sunday and out for a little stroll.

'Hi!' I say, as if I am surprised to see him.

'Hi,' he says grinning.

'Why don't you take a suitcase? It must be terrible getting all your stuff in a rucksack,' I say.

Ash shakes his head and says, 'Don't ask . . . You know how Dad likes to do everything the hard way.'

He's wearing his dog T-shirt again. I stare at it rather self-consciously.

'You look nice, are you going out?' he asks, sliding the box he is holding into the boot and then standing and staring at me.

I look away, suddenly shy. I feel a bit of a fool now because I have washed my hair and put make-up on and got dressed in my smartest jeans and second-best T-shirt. I don't know how to tell him that the thought of him being away for a whole week is terrible, that I shall miss him, and I want his last view of me to be of a pretty smiling face.

'I suppose I normally look like a dog's dinner in the morning,' I say.

'Yep, but not today,' he says laughing.

'Before you start in with the insults—here's a present. Don't come back like a famine victim. I need you fit and strong to help me with the dreaded cousins,' I joke, as I hold out a giant Yorkie bar and huge Toblerone that I have been hiding behind my back. 'You can share them with your dad. I thought they might last you a week . . .'

'Two weeks . . .'

'Two weeks . . .' I echo. I can feel my face falling. I try to look surprised rather than upset.

'Dad is so keen on the bivvying idea that we are going up to Scotland. They've got bigger mountains and real wilderness up there evidently. He's managed to get a decent locum in—so he feels he can take a bit more leave. And he's decided the Lakes are a bit tame.'

'Oh, you poor thing . . .' I say. But the truth is I am the poor thing, not him. How shall I manage without him? Ellen is away too. I shall have to cope with Crystal with no one to moan to, or ask for advice.

'I'll text you . . .' he says.

'Yes,' I say miserably. 'I'll have to get some credit for my phone.'

'You shouldn't have bothered . . . with the chocolate,' he says. 'But thanks.'

I thrust the chocolate bars into his hands. 'I'll miss you,' I mutter.

'I'll miss you too,' he says quietly.

He takes a step forward. I take a step forward. I am on a level with the dog and the slogan on his T-shirt. 'A friend is for life—not just for Christmas,' I say. It's a feeble joke. I swallow hard. I wish I was a dog. I'd jump into the back of their Volvo and refuse to get out. More than anything in the world I want to turn the clock back and not have the cousins here and get in the car with him and Ralph. Bivvying—Scotland—camping in a swamp with crocodiles—anything seems preferable to being stuck here without him to talk to—especially as the threat of Crystal messing up my life is hanging over me.

'Take care of yourself. I'll bring you back a haggis. They make lovely pets,' he says.

'You have a good time . . .' I mutter. I reach out and give him a hug and feel again the well-washed softness of his old T-shirt against my face. He dips his head and kisses me. His mouth lands somewhere between my ear and my nose—but even so it's lovely. Just for a moment we are frozen: him with his hands full of chocolate bars, me holding on to his T-shirt like a little kid desperate for a cuddle.

'Good morning, Rose!' Ralph booms from the coach house doorway and we spring apart.

'Hi, have a good holiday. See you when you get back. If there's anything you want us to do for you while you are away—just ring. Have a good time. Bye . . .' I talk too quickly as I make my escape.

Bolting through the kitchen door I nearly collide with Crystal. I can tell by the silly look on her face that she has been watching us. Glancing at the window I see that the calico is flapping.

She begins to giggle. 'I thought he was quite cute at first—even if he is a ginga—but he's a useless kisser. Was the chocolate a bribe? I should ask for your money back.'

'Why don't you shut up?' I say fiercely.

She starts to laugh; for some reason the sound seems to go right through my head. 'Shut up!' I warn.

'You must be desperate to be chasing him,' she giggles. 'What a plonker!'

'I'm not chasing him. He's my friend,' I say with an attempt at dignity because I can feel my temper rising up like a pressure cooker.

'Oh yeah . . . You were begging for it . . .' she sniggers. 'Begging for a snog with a big ginger plonker.'

'Shut up!' I howl, and I spring across and make her stop by giving her a crack across the face with the flat of my hand.

She doesn't cry. Her hand comes up and covers the red patch on her cheek. Her eyes are dark and glittering like those of an angry rodent. 'You'll be sorry you did that,' she threatens. 'I'll make you sorry for that . . .' she says again.

I'm sorry already, but I'm not going to let her see it. My mother doesn't believe in physical violence and would be absolutely horrified at what I have just done. Also, I can't remember the last time I got in a physical fight with anyone. It must have been very early on in junior school. I am shocked and sickened by my actions. I *am* sorry. But I am also full of rage towards Crystal. It is her fault—she made me do it.

'I don't know why they bothered to call you Crystal. Broken Glass would have been a better name. You are so ugly and sordid. You bring everything down to your disgusting level. Get out of my sight!' I rant.

She faces up to me. Her lower lip curls. If she was a dog she would be rabid. She is one hell of a mean kid.

'And I don't know why they bothered to call you Rose,' she snaps back, quick as a flash. She's obviously more used than me to verbal combat and the delicate art of abuse. 'Thorn would have been a better name for you,' she adds triumphantly. 'Spiky, mean thorn,' she jeers. 'Who can't get a boyfriend. And we all know why. Because she's about as sexy as cat sick.'

'Oh, you'd know all about cat sick, wouldn't you?' I reply. I can hear how immature and stupid I sound. I shall have to get away from her before I start to cry.

I go up to my room, lock the door, and curl under my eiderdown. I only allow myself the release of crying when my head is right under my pillow. I would die rather than let Broken Glass hear how she has upset me.

9

It begins to rain and it isn't light summer rain or warm drizzle. This is a monsoon lashing, dark with the curse of the Himalayas, and it falls in harsh lines from a black sky. It crushes our garden—flowers, weeds, unsteady bushes, and tree branches all collapse under the cold weight of the onslaught. And all this bleak destruction seems to echo my mood. I feel as if my life is under threat from alien forces—namely Broken Glass. I don't know how I shall cope until the end of the holidays.

Life is stressful on every front—the slates and chimneys of our house, elderly, leaky, and complaining, go into the roofing equivalent of cardiac arrest. Fountains spurt, watercourses emerge, and networks of springs erupt all over the attic. It's hell: bloody, watery hell, and there is no sensible Ash or competent Ralph to call on to help us.

For days Mum and I race up and down stairs with buckets and saucepans, margarine containers, ornamental vases, anything which will hold water. It's a hopeless job: the containers overflow, we trip and drop things in our haste, and it seems that water is everywhere. There are damp patches on ceilings, mould on walls. The house is like a sponge . . . Mum is tearful. I am cross. When Broken Glass helps she moves like a slug. I'd like to stamp on her—but even the help of a slug is better than nothing at all.

The only good thing about the crisis is that Mum is so taken up with it that she doesn't notice the terrible arctic atmosphere between me and Crystal.

Hamish arrives with the storms. He's come back from Scotland early to look at the roof. It's raining cats and dogs in Scotland, he says, and the long range forecast is really terrible. I think about Ash and wish I could talk to him. There's no phone network where he is so I don't know if he's drowning or drying out in a hotel somewhere.

Water doesn't seem to bother Hamish. He dons waterproofs and goes up a ladder to watch the gutters overflowing and splashes about outside looking in drains. Then he spends a morning in the attic, emptying buckets, whistling cheerfully, and looking at sodden roof timbers. He says that it's easier to work out what is wrong with a roof when it's actually leaking.

I am quite pleased really when he turns up every day. Mum is much less stressed when he is around. And I have to admit that having someone else in the house— even Hamish MacCrimmon—seems to make everything more cheerful.

And I have to be grateful for any little help in lifting the complete gloom that has overtaken me. In the past Ellen and I have done masses of quizzes in girls' mags and I have always come out as really optimistic and extrovert. But I don't feel like that any more. I feel terrible. It's not just the awfulness of having B-Glass in my home. Thankfully our house is big enough for us to avoid each other most of the time. The worst thing is missing Ash so much. It's been so bad that sometimes I have felt as if some important part of me has disappeared. It has been like living with only one hand or one foot. I keep remembering a sad line from a song: 'What's the sound of one hand clapping?' because that sums up how I feel. I hadn't realized how much I have got to rely on him. So having anyone at all in the house to break up all this misery is good. It's made me feel quite kindly towards Hamish.

'How does Hamish know so much about roofs and

things like that?' I ask Mum while we are in the kitchen making sandwiches for lunch.

'Hamish worked as a labourer on building sites in Glasgow when he was young,' Mum says cheerfully, as if this is something rather wonderful. I suppose, when your roof is leaking as badly as ours, it is rather wonderful to have someone around who knows about these things. Although I am sure Ralph would have helped with the roof—because he is sure to be as competent about DIY as he is about everything else.

'So how did he get into poetry?' I ask, dipping a crust into the jar of mayonnaise and eating it. Since Ash has been away I've done nothing but comfort eat. I simply can't wait for lunch. 'Bit of a contrast to labouring, isn't it?' I add. Mum has got three of Hamish's books of poetry on her desk; she says he's tipped to be Laureate one day. He's obviously an exceptionally good poet.

'It was a spell in prison when he was young that turned him around. He's a phoenix. Out of the dust of his old life rose a new and better one . . .' Mum says, and her voice is gentle with pride. You'd think she was talking about me.

'Prison . . .' I can't keep the horror out of my voice.

'Yes, I thought you knew . . . it's in his biographical notes on the book cover . . .' Mum looks startled at my shock.

'Mum, I don't think you should have him here all the time . . . We haven't got Ralph next door at the moment for protection.'

'Rose, what on earth are you talking about?' Mum looks as if she doesn't know whether to laugh or cry. I feel unreasonably upset. Surely I don't have to spell this out to her. She's the one who has always been so security conscious.

'I know you have to work with him at the university and everything. But you must be able to see that having him here in the house when he's a person like that isn't a good thing.'

'Rose, for heaven's sake! He wasn't a sex offender or anything terrible like that!' Mum's face is suddenly scarlet. 'Do give me credit for a bit of sense!'

'Well, what did he do, then, to be sent to prison? It can't have been for helping old ladies across the road,' I say.

Mum looks a bit stricken. 'It was a fight. There are lots of tribal loyalties in Glasgow. His brother was attacked and Hamish got hold of the attacker's knife and retaliated. He's the first to admit he was no angel and was in the wrong. But he never armed himself with the intention of harming others. It was a spur of the moment act of rage.'

'Oh, I suppose that makes it all right then,' I say rather helplessly. 'What happened to the other person?'

'He recovered but was badly scarred. Hamish isn't proud of what he did—but it's in the past now. He has a new life. He's a different person. He started to study when he was in prison . . . that was the beginning. It was over twenty years ago, Rose.'

'Well—I hope he gets the roof sorted out quickly,' I say. 'How awful . . .'

'I thought you liked him,' Mum says miserably.

'He's OK . . .' I say. 'And it's nice that he helps you with your poems.'

'Rose . . . I . . .' Mum starts to say.

'And it's very kind of him to help us with the roof,' I add. 'But you can't be too careful, Mum. You've always said how vulnerable women who are on their own are, haven't you?'

'Yes,' she mutters.

'He's not someone like Ralph, is he?' I point out gently. 'Someone we've known and liked for years—someone who we know everything about.'

'I don't think it's possible to ever really know the human heart—not even our own. "To delve the secret darkness of a soul and find a flickering flame of truth . . ." We all hide behind the person we would like to be. "I wear a mask to show I am of the human race . . ."' Mum quotes softly. The tuna and salad lie forgotten on the table. Her hands are still and there is a faraway look in her eyes. She is lost in the thoughts inside her head.

I've always really loved the way she talks in poems. But today I find it strangely irritating.

'Not everyone is like that,' I say firmly. 'Some people are just what they seem. Look at Ash and Ralph. They don't hide anything. What you see is what you get. Ralph doesn't have any skeletons in his past. And he has always said if you need a hand with anything to give him a shout. And look how good he was with Cara when you did ask for help. And he was always offering to do the garden for you, wasn't he? I am sure he would have mended the boiler and helped with the roof. He would have been happy to do it.'

'Yes, I'm sure you are right. He is very kind . . .' Mum mumbles. 'But he works such long hours . . .'

'He has loads of energy. Look at all the jogging and swimming he does to fill up his time. It really would be a kindness to let him help out with things . . . He likes to feel needed and useful. He's always offering, isn't he? Or he used to. But you were always so chippy with him,' I grumble.

'I wasn't chippy, or I didn't intend to be,' Mum says sadly. 'But I value my independence.'

'Not much point being independent when the house is falling apart. I think you need all the help you can get—from Ralph, that is.'

'We could sell up, Rose. Even in this state the house would go for quite a lot of money. We could buy somewhere small, get a car. It won't be long before you will want driving lessons, a car of your own, university fees . . . Maybe it's wrong and sentimental to cling on to the past like this. Aunt May didn't intend for the house to be an albatross around my neck . . . I'm sure.'

'Mum, you are not the Ancient Mariner, and the house is not a burden. It just needs a bit of repair. And I would curl up and die if we had to leave. I love living here. I love the house and I love living next door to Ralph and Ash. I couldn't manage if we lived anywhere else . . .' I feel quite tearful at the thought of not coming home from school with Ash any more—which is what I have been doing since Year 7. It would mean the end of our cosy after-school chats and him helping me with my homework.

'Please don't talk about selling the house,' I beg and my eyes fill with tears.

'All right, don't get upset,' Mum says quickly. 'I didn't realize . . . I mean I know you love living here . . . but I didn't realize quite how attached you are. Also we need the space because I'm not sure what is going to happen with Cara and Crystal. If Milo doesn't come back we may have them here for a while.'

'Not after the holidays have finished?' I mumble. I am terrified of looking at Mum in case she sees the horror on my face. 'But they can't stay here with us . . .' I blurt out.

'Jasmine has a long contract on cruise ships. Milo says it was the only way for her to make any money. If he doesn't get his CD finished and come back to England and provide a home for them they will have to stay here with us . . . I can't very well hand them over to the social services. We'll have to get them enrolled at a school and make the best of it. I've been discussing it with Hamish.'

'But we've got ages yet!' I yelp.

'Oh, darling, the summer holidays go so quickly . . . I need to get in touch with schools . . . sort out uniforms . . . that sort of thing—it can't all be left to the last minute . . .'

'Mum,' I say desperately. 'You'll have to get in touch with Milo and tell him he's got to come back for them. They simply can't stay here with us. It's impossible!'

Something of my panic seems to filter through to Mum.

'Darling! I thought you liked having them here. I thought they were the little sisters you never had. Cara adores you—she follows you around like a devoted puppy and you seem so fond of her.'

'It's all right for the holidays . . .' I mutter. 'But a little of them goes a long way . . .' I don't like to say that adoration comes at a price. It's all right Cara being my shadow while Ash is away but what will happen when he's back? Ash and I won't be able to have a proper grown-up conversation with her hanging around me all the time.

'We may not have a choice . . .' Mum says sadly. 'We will have to see it through to the end, Rose. I'm sorry.'

'Not as sorry as me . . .' I mutter as I leave the room. I go upstairs and throw myself down on my bed. The truth is I have been counting the days until the end of the holidays. I want life to go back to me and Ash and Ellen hanging out together. I want to forget all about Josh and crushes and cousins and dance shows.

'Oh, Ash,' I whisper into my pillow. 'Come back from bivvying soon and save me . . .'

The rain eases on the first day of rehearsals. This is a relief because neither Cara nor Crystal has a proper raincoat. Cara has a little pink anorak and Crystal a silver puffa jacket. I have a waterproof but it is really old and leaky. As it is we manage to get down to the Academy with a couple of umbrellas and get only a bit damp.

'Now, I need you to be a help,' I explain to Cara. 'I take a warm-up in this studio and then the groups go into Mrs Valente to rehearse. I also have to mark everyone who arrives and leaves so I'm very busy.'

'And bossy,' Crystal mutters, but I ignore this.

'Now you can join in the warm-up or you can sit in the cloakroom and look at a book. But you mustn't go anywhere without telling me. No one is allowed to wander outside or go onto the fire escape or leave rehearsals without being signed out.'

'Welcome to jail,' Crystal says.

'It's important because we have lots of little ones and Mrs Valente is responsible for them while they are here at the Academy. We can't risk anyone getting lost,' I explain to Cara. I turn to Crystal and say icily, 'The rules apply to you too, you know.'

Crystal ignores me—but Cara gives me a hug and says, 'I'll stay here with you. And I'll help you.'

'Yes! You can help,' I say gratefully. 'Because you have lovely toes and can show some of the really little babies how to have good toes.'

'Do some of them have naughty toes?' Cara asks delightedly.

'Oh yes, some of them are very little, and have terribly naughty toes. You can be very kind to them. Hold their hands and show them good toes and help them to skip.'

Crystal raises her eyes to heaven at all this baby talk but we take no notice. Cara and I like each other. We like talking about dancing and being friends and Crystal can't spoil it. Cara's really thrilled with her practice clothes. She's tried them on endlessly at home and now today at the studio she is bursting with pride. I've put her hair in two little plaits and she looks really sweet.

Because I organize the rotas I have put Crystal into Amelia's group so I don't have to do warm-up with her. We are not dancing in any of the same numbers so I shouldn't see much of her. Thank goodness.

What really is unfair is that Crystal looks wonderful in practice clothes. She has a natural dancer's figure: long legs, slim thighs, a lithe back, and a graceful neck.

Cara is a good little dancer with lovely feet. She can really point her toes, so I am curious about Crystal's ability. At the end of the week I ask Amelia if Crystal is any good.

'Well, she's got a marvellous turn-out,' Amelia says.

'It's strange because she moves beautifully as if she should be good, but when she starts dancing she is very wooden and sulky with no projection at all.'

'Her mother is a dancer so I should imagine that is why she looks the part. But Crystal says she hates dancing,' I say.

'What a waste . . .' Amelia says. 'I wish you could do body swaps. I'd have her thighs. I've been going to bed with my legs wrapped in cling film but it doesn't seem to help.'

I am too busy to reply. The morning has been hectic, with some children turning up at the wrong time and missing their rehearsal. I want to get everyone out of the door so we can have our lunch. Amelia and I bring sandwiches and are allowed into the staff kitchen to make drinks. I have special permission for Crystal and Cara to stay too and I have made us our usual picnic of Marmite sandwiches, bananas, and Penguin biscuits. I've been working really hard and I am ravenous.

As soon as I walk into the kitchen my nose is assaulted by the most glorious smell. My hungry stomach does a triple somersault. But then anxiety flares. Mrs Valente has gone out to do her weekly shop and Amelia has been whisked off to the BHS café by her mother to have the slimmer's special. There is no one here but me and Crystal and Cara. So how come the kitchen smells divinely of pizza?

The fire door is open. I crash through. Crystal is sitting on the top step of the fire escape basking in sunlight. On her lap is a pizza box. She is stuffing a slice into her mouth. It's pepperoni and pineapple. The sight and smell of it makes me feel sick with hunger and rage and disbelief.

'What the bloody hell do you think you are doing?' I snap.

'What does it look like, stupid? I'm having my lunch . . .' Crystal says airily. She picks a succulent piece of green pepper from the pizza and pops it in her mouth. Her sharp dark eyes stare at me insolently as she chews and swallows. Then she smiles tauntingly at me. It's as if she knows I am hungry and my mouth is damp with longing.

Cara has followed me out through the open fire door. 'Oh goody, pizza. It's ages and ages since we had pizza. Let me . . .' She tries to push past me but I shove her back into the kitchen.

'Get in here,' I bark at Crystal. I grab her and haul her into the kitchen. 'There are notices everywhere saying that no one must open the fire doors or go out onto the fire escape. That's one rule you have broken. And you must have gone out to get that pizza. You weren't signed out—were you?'

'Oh, get real, does it really matter?' Crystal says. 'I didn't get abducted or run over by a bus. And it's too nice a day to sit indoors. If I have another Marmite sandwich I'll throw up. I wanted something different today and I know that old Fanny Valente is out. Look, there's enough for all of us,' she adds, holding the box out to me. 'Have a piece . . .' she says. 'Go on . . .'

'And where did you get the money to buy it?' I say appalled. It's a deep pan, full size, with loads of extras. It must have cost a fortune.

'Auntie Hal is always saying there's money in the teapot . . .' Crystal says.

'She says that to me—not to you!' I say through gritted teeth. I am so angry that every muscle in my body is tense. 'How dare you!'

'Auntie Hal does say it to us. And pizza is nice . . .' Cara whines suddenly. She is creeping past me—going over to join Crystal—drawn to the sight and smell of the pizza. She leans over and takes a slice and begins to cram it into her mouth. 'Have some, Rose . . . it's gorgeous,' she adds, with her mouth full. She's got little bits of cheesy tomato dribbling down her chin. She's going at it as if she is a hungry little dog. The sight of her revolts me. My stomach starts to spin with nausea and sharp hunger pains.

For a moment I feel really dangerous. As if I might explode with rage, grab the pizza, and throw it at them. Then my phone rings. Like a robot I glance down at the number. It's Ash. I bolt out of the room and run as far away from them as I can.

Ash asks me how I am and I can't stop myself. Everything that is happening here with the cousins comes out in a rush—one long sentence full of rage and misery.

I finally stop and wait for him to make me feel better. But he doesn't. He says, 'I'd always thought the Academy summer show sounded like a boot camp. And now I know it is. Be reasonable, Rose, you can't expect Crystal to toe the line for you. She's probably been used to being in charge of Cara and doing exactly what she wants in London. See it from her point of view. And don't lose your temper or you'll make it worse. Once she knows how to wind you up she'll never stop.'

'Thanks a lot,' I say biting back my tears and glad that he hasn't got a video-phone.

'I'm on your side,' he says. 'But you'll have to use some psychology and outsmart her.'

'What should I do?' I wail.

'Have a piece of pizza and take them out for a bit. Not everyone wants to spend their life stuck at the Academy thinking about dancing like you do. Where do they like to go?'

'The Internet café . . .' I mumble.

'Well, take them there. Lighten up a bit. Don't keep on about the rules and regulations as if you are the Gestapo. You'll just make them rebel. You know what a stroppy little madam Crystal is. Get her on your side.'

'OK . . .' I say bravely. 'I'll try to do it your way.'

'I'm missing you like crazy, Rosie,' he says, and the line must have gone fuzzy because his voice sounds really gruff.

'Oh, Ash,' I wail. 'I'm missing you too. I'm counting the days, no . . . not just the days, the minutes until you come back . . .'

'Are you really?' he asks.

'Honestly!'

He laughs and I laugh too. 'You've made me feel loads better,' I say. 'Thank you.'

'I better go. I'll try to ring you tonight,' he says. 'Take care . . .'

I feel dreadful when the line goes dead because I realize that I have talked the whole time about myself and my problems, and never asked him once how he is. Their tent might have got washed away or he could be starving to death up there in Scotland . . . But he sounded cheerful enough—and it was so brilliant to talk to him that I find I am irrationally happy.

I go into the kitchen and lock the fire door.

'We saved you a piece of pizza,' Cara says. They are both looking a bit guilty and worried.

'Thanks,' I say. The pizza is cold now and rather congealed but I eat it anyway as a token of reconciliation. 'Shall we go out for a while as it isn't raining?' I suggest.

Crystal looks at me a bit suspiciously, but I manage a tight kind of smile. They get their coats, I munch a squashy Marmite sandwich (and wish it was another slice of pizza), and we set off for town.

10

We are just turning into the main street, fighting our way through the lunchtime crush of tourists and shoppers, when I hear someone shouting my name. It's so crowded that at first I can't make out who is calling me. Then I see Reece Browne, smiling and waving as if I am a long-lost relative. Jessica and Josh are standing next to him: Jessica is giving me a dead-eye look that wouldn't disgrace a cod fish—and Josh is looking mean, moody, and magnificent in American jeans and surfing T-shirt. Even though I tell myself that Josh is horrible and I hate him, I can't stop a little thrill of delight running down my spine. He is just so good looking.

'Who the hell is that?' Crystal whispers. 'Oh-my-god-he's-drop-dead-gorgeous! Don't tell me you know him?'

'What?' I say a bit irritably. Reece is making his way over to me with Jessica and Josh trailing behind him reluctantly. Crystal is rooted to the ground, eyes bright with expectation, while Cara is pulling at my hand and moaning that she is hungry. There is no chance of pretending I haven't seen the Brownes and moving on quickly. I start to feel harassed. I am also really embarrassed. My face is clear of make-up, my hair is pulled back in a scrunchy, and I am wearing my leotard, crossover, and jazz trousers. I had banked on slipping into town and not seeing anyone at all. And just to make it all a thousand million times more humiliating the Brownes are all tanned and trendy in designer denims and cool tops. They must have gone away for the first two weeks of the holidays and are now back ready to show off their film-star looks to the rest of the world.

'Hi, Rose. How are you? Are you having a good holiday?' Reece is so pleased to see me I almost expect to be swept into his arms and kissed. 'Have you heard from Ellen?' he asks excitedly.

'I've had a postcard,' I mumble. 'She's on safari in Kenya.'

'I know,' he says happily. 'We went two years ago and it was great—especially seeing lions. I really hope she's having a good time.'

I start to hope that he won't ask about my holiday plans. It would be too awful to have to confess in front of Josh that I'm a boring stay-at-home, and the only big cat I am likely to be seeing is next-door's tabby. But Reece seems more concerned that I might walk away and leave him talking to himself. He's got me boxed in and is gabbling fast, like a double-glazing salesman.

'It's great to see you, Rose. We're off to Monty's to sort out my birthday party. I hope you and Ellen and Ash will be able to come along to it. It's a week on Saturday. Ellen is back by then,' he adds with a grin.

'Yes,' I say a bit distantly. I wonder how he knows so much about Ellen's plans. He's talking about her as if she's his best friend, not mine.

'Are these your cousins? Ellen told me they were staying with you,' Reece asks. 'Hi,' he says to Crystal, and gets a beaming smile in return. 'Will you still be here for my party?' he asks. 'Come along with Rose and Ellen if you are.'

'Great, thanks, I'd love to,' Crystal says, casual as anything. Just as if she is always being invited out to places like Monty's—which is the coolest nightclub in the city.

Cara pulls at my hand and whispers: 'Will I be able to go to the party, Rosie? Will you take me?'

I ignore her, because this request is just too stupid.

But Reece crouches down so his face is on a level with hers. 'I'm really sorry,' he says sincerely. 'But you're a bit too young. It's for thirteen to seventeen year olds only.'

Cara's face falls and her bottom lip pouts. 'That's not fair,' she grumbles.

Reece smiles at her sympathetically. 'I'm sorry. I'll tell you what,' he adds kindly. 'How about if we all go to Nelson's now and have ice cream as a special early b'day treat for me? Have you had your lunch? Because they do wicked potato wedges there. I've got a load of birthday money—so it's my shout. Will you come, please, Rose?'

I'm really embarrassed because Nelson's is mega expensive. And I have been so unfailingly cool to Reece in the past that I can't believe he's offering to take me and the cousins there just because a little kid like Cara can't go to his party.

'Oh, I don't think so . . .' I start to say.

'Please—Jess and Josh are bored stiff with talking about my party. Come and tell me what you think I should have. You can have themed or fancy dress at Monty's and I've got to decide on the food and make a list of people to invite. Come and have an ice cream or a coffee and give me the benefit of your advice.' Reece grins at me with such kindness I don't feel I can say 'No'.

Suddenly I understand why Ellen likes him. If he was a dog he'd be a huge-pawed hound that licks your face and leaps around you and makes you feel like a million dollars. It's impossible not to warm to him.

He puts his hand out to Cara and she takes hold of it. 'We had pizza for lunch—but Crystal ate loads of it—and then I had to save a piece for Rosie—and I am absolutely starving,' she blurts out breathlessly. Honestly, to hear the child you would think she never got fed. There's a whole pile of sandwiches waiting for us at the Academy.

'You've got your packed lunch to eat when we get back,' I remind her.

'I'm sick of Marmite and I'm hungry now,' Cara says stubbornly.

'That's good, because I'm ravenous,' Reece says gleefully. 'Jess is dieting and Josh has a hangover so they are no fun to lunch with. You and me will get wedges with chilli and mayo dip and have banana splits for afters. We'll have a complete pig-out, shall we?' he says to Cara.

'Oh yes. I love pigging out. I'm a piggy in the show, you know . . .' Cara says happily.

We get shown to the big window table at Nelson's. It has been an ambition of mine to sit there and watch the world go by (and hopefully be seen by the world). I can't believe that I'm doing it now in my practice clothes and no make-up.

It's just as well that Cara and Reece are chattering away as if they are bestest friends because Jessica is silent, Crystal is studying the menu, and Josh is sprawling back in his chair with his shades hiding his eyes. He's acting as if being with us is such a bore he might as well go to sleep.

I make a conscious effort not to look at him and turn my attention to the gorgeous food on offer. The prices make me wince and I try to order something cheap. But Reece is unstoppable. He insists that we all have wedges and then ice creams. All except Jess and Josh—they both insist on nothing but black coffee.

If I wasn't already so embarrassed about how I look I would be embarrassed by the amount of food which Crystal and Cara put away. Reece orders Cara the biggest Knickerbocker Glory on the menu and she dives at it and spoons it into her mouth as if she's never had ice cream before. Actually, I'm not doing too badly myself because Reece keeps on ordering extra stuff: strawberries and warm chocolate cookies; and I am tucking in.

'My God! You can eat! Where on earth do you put it?' Josh says to me. I look up to find he has taken off his shades and is staring hard at me. I had been so taken up with the loveliness of the biscuits and the huge mugs of cappuccino that I had quite forgotten he was there.

'I've been dancing all morning; it's extremely hard work,' I say a bit abruptly. I don't want anything to distract me from this lovely feast. He's obviously in a foul mood.

'You must have hollow legs, there's not an ounce of fat on you.' His eyes linger on me for so long I feel my face start to heat. I lift my mug of coffee and try not to look at him. He turns to his sister. 'Maybe you should take up dancing, Jess, get rid of your middle-age spread and fat arse.'

Jessica's smooth face puckers for a moment, which is the nearest she gets to a frown.

For some reason he really annoys me by talking about being fat. It's boring. Everyone at the Academy is obsessed by how they look because it really matters for dancers. I don't want to hear about it while I am at Nelson's having a divine pig-out. And anyway, Jessica is built like a beanpole.

'Don't be so ridiculous,' I snap. 'Jess's got a great figure and she's tall. She could be a model.'

Jessica flashes me a grateful glance but Josh sneers and says, 'She's got cellulite on her legs and bum droop. And American boys notice things like that—don't they, Jess?' he adds maliciously.

She stares out of the window and doesn't reply, but I can see from her eyes that she is hurt.

Josh grins. He's enjoying winding her up. I think back to the party and how small and hurt he made me feel. He may be the best-looking boy in the world but he talks shit.

'And what about American girls? Are they as shallow as the boys and obsessed with physical perfection?' I ask with mock innocence. 'Let's hope not—appearances can be so deceptive, can't they? Some people seem to think how you look is the most important thing in the world—

when really it's what kind of person you are that matters. There's no point in being fantastically good-looking but having a crap personality—is there?'

Josh stares at me without replying and Jessica giggles. I meet Josh's eyes and refuse to look away. He gives in first and looks down at his coffee and begins to stir it.

I move my chair so I am turned away from him. He is gorgeous and I don't want to admire him more than I have to. I wish I wasn't so attracted to him. I could stare at him for hours. There is something about the sharp lines of his face and his blond spiky hair that makes me want to sit and drink him in. But, at the same time, I know I am drawn to him against my better judgement. It's like longing for cream cakes—you know they won't taste as good as they look, but you still crave the taste of cream and chocolate on your lips however empty the aftertaste may be. I know he is going to hate me now for talking back to him, but I tell myself I don't care. He's never going to fancy me the way I fancy him . . . is he?

While I am talking to Reece I am aware of Josh staring at me. But Reece doesn't give anyone else a chance to talk to me. He is sweet. He asks my opinion on everything. You'd think it was my party not his. Everything I suggest he thinks is wonderful. We decide on a celebrity theme—which means people can dress up as much or as little as they want—and make a list of suitable food.

It's Crystal who tugs at my sleeve and reminds me of the time. 'Thanks a lot for lunch. It's been great. We'll have to dash or we'll be late for rehearsal . . .' I say to Reece, as I wipe Cara's sticky face with a napkin.

'See you at the party . . .' he says to Crystal, as she mutters her thanks.

'Crystal's not old enough to go to Reece's party, is she?' Cara says to me as we walk down the street.

'No . . . But she looks older and she'll enjoy it, won't she?' I say, in what I hope is a neutral tone. It was on the tip of my tongue to tell Reece that Crystal is only eleven and therefore couldn't possibly go along to the party. In truth the last thing in the world I want is to take her out with me, Ash, and Ellen. But I decided to take Ash's advice and avoid confrontation with her—and it does seem to have worked. Crystal could easily have let me go nattering on and be late for rehearsal but she didn't—and that was decent of her. Amelia and I are working on *Beauty and the Beast* this afternoon and it's really important that I am warmed-up and ready.

'Can I come and watch you and Amelia?' Cara asks.

'Yes, if you would like to. But you'll have to sit very quietly.' I'm a bit edgy about these rehearsals for *Beauty and the Beast*. Amelia and I are the two top seniors and our number is the finale and the most important in the show. Also, when there are only two of you on stage, there's no room for mistakes.

'I'll be like a little mouse,' she promises. 'I love to see you dancing, Rosie,' she adds, squeezing my hand.

To my surprise Crystal comes into the studio with Cara. Normally Crystal sits in the cloakroom and plays on her Game Boy unless she is called for a rehearsal. It puts me off for the first few minutes having her sitting watching me with her dark inscrutable eyes. I have to make a conscious effort to lose myself in what we are doing.

Amelia and I have learnt the steps, now we have to give the parts interpretation and emotion. Beauty dances on pointe and the Beast in bare feet. I am really envious of Amelia's part because it's the male role and is very fast and gutsy—also I adore working in bare feet. Ballet and especially pointe work is my least favourite and I have to work really hard at it. During the dance Beauty is by turns timid and loving towards the Beast and I find it quite difficult to think myself into the part. Being angry and tortured would be far easier for me.

We work on my solo and then our pas de deux. I

manage to get through it all without a mistake; although my ankle wobbles a bit on the last arabesque. And all the time I am aware of Crystal watching me with concentration—her eyes are like X-rays. I suppose she's hoping I will fall flat on my face.

'Well done, girls,' Mrs Valente says. 'Amelia, that was very good, but your jetés will have to be improved. The Beast is a wild thing so when you spring we must believe that you might leap into the audience. And, Rose—you will have to work on being fragile, you must loosen up those posé turns, they must be part of your fight to get away from the Beast.'

We are left to work alone. I had hoped that Crystal would leave as well but she stays, watching me all the time with the same intense interest as if she is a mad scientist and I am a specimen. I'm pretty fed up. Having her in the room makes me feel spooked.

When we get home there is great excitement. A small parcel has arrived from America. It is addressed to Mum but she has waited to open it until we've come back. I say a silent and very heartfelt prayer of thanks that at last the money has arrived and I can pay Mrs Valente. What a weight off my mind!

Mum gives the parcel to Crystal to open. 'I expect it's an early birthday present for you . . .' she says.

'When is it your birthday?' I ask.

'In two weeks,' she mutters. Her normally pale face is flushed and her hands shake slightly as she tears at the brown paper envelope.

Cara is gabbling away to Mum—telling her all about the excitement of being taken to a café by Reece and having ice cream. But I am studying Crystal. Her face is tense as she empties the contents of the envelope onto the table. There is a layer of paper—not birthday parcel wrapping—just the kind of white tissue that expensive shops put around clothes. Crystal scrabbles. There are three T-shirts inside and a note written on a scrap of paper torn from a writing pad. 'Thought you'd like these—speak soon—love D.'

There is no letter—no separate envelope with money inside—no cheque or money order tucked inside the clothes. He's simply bought three T-shirts from some exclusive New York shop, put them in a brown envelope, and sent them off to us by air mail.

'Aren't they beautiful? What a lovely surprise,' Mum says, holding them up one by one, her long sensitive fingers touching the material gently. 'They are pure silk and so pretty. Look—this is yours, Cara—pink with a butterfly on the front. And Crystal's is green with a dragon. And how clever, do look, Rose, yours is black with scarlet roses. Aren't they lovely!' she repeats again, as if puzzled by my and Crystal's lack of enthusiasm. We are staring down at the T-shirts with blank expressions. In contrast Mum's face is soft and smiling as she adds, 'Milo has always been good at buying presents. He's so generous.' She doesn't seem to have noticed that he hasn't sent her anything or enclosed the money he promised her.

'Mine's the prettiest, isn't it, Auntie Hal? Daddy bought it specially for me because he knows butterflies are my favourite. Can I try it on?' Cara cries delightedly.

'Of course you can, dear,' Mum says. And she helps Cara take off her practice clothes and slides the silky T-shirt over her head.

While Mum isn't looking I shake out the tissue paper and peer inside the brown envelope—hoping against hope that there might be something else hidden inside. Praying futilely for a cheque—or a huge wad of dollars—or even a small wad of dollars . . . anything that would help pay Mrs Valente's bill. It's driving me nuts going to rehearsals every day knowing I still owe for the costumes and practice clothes. But the envelope is completely empty.

I am choked full of misery and, when I glance up, I

see a similar expression on Crystal's face. It should make me feel better to know that she is as unhappy as me— but it doesn't. Her being upset is likely to make her even more difficult to live with. And I still have the problem of how to pay Mrs Valente's bill.

11

Hamish makes a map of the roof. It's really beautiful. (I tell him it will end up in the Tate Modern, which makes him laugh.) It is colour coded: red shows roof tiles that have slipped or need replacing, orange is for flashing that needs renewing around the chimney pots, and green shows trees that are too close to the house and need to be cut down. There are other colours for drainpipes and gutters and there are so many hues and lines that it really does look like an abstract painting.

Mum gazes at it in horror. I can see trouble ahead. It's not the amount of work that needs doing—that's bad enough—it's the trees. No one in the world (not even a poet) would object to having their gutters sorted out—and it really isn't possible to be emotionally involved with a drainpipe—but the trees are different. Mum is very fond of the trees.

'I can't see how the trees in the garden would cause water to drip down inside the house,' she says. 'The trees are so beautiful and make the house so lovely and private. No one can see in.'

Hamish explains lots of technical stuff about how some of the trees were planted too close to the house and not pruned back, so over the years they have grown too big. As he talks he stabs on the map with his pencil.

I'm not really listening, but I hear Mum exclaim, 'Oh, but Aunt May planted those two little fir trees when she was a girl. I couldn't possibly have them cut down. It would be sacrilege.'

'They're not little fir trees, Mum,' I say. 'They are taller than the house. And they make the front room really cold and dark—when by rights it ought to be the sunniest room in the house.'

'The front room is fine,' Mum says stubbornly. 'I'd hate to change the garden—it's always been like this. I remember so clearly when Milo and I visited Aunt May when we were children. It was such a magical place . . . And it all seemed so huge to me then: giant rhododendron bushes and a shrubbery you could get lost in, but of course it was just an ordinary garden. I'm sure it's not the trees . . .' she says beseechingly to Hamish.

Hamish explains slowly and carefully, drawing little diagrams, about how the tree branches fill the gutters— which means they overflow and the water runs down the outside walls of the house. There is also the problem that when it's windy the big branches knock against the slates and dislodge them. There's quite a lot of physics involved in his explanation (my least favourite subject in the world) but even I can see it makes sense. The roof does leak where the trees are—even a baby could see that from the diagram.

But Mum doesn't want to know. She gets red flushes of colour in the cheeks of her normally pale face and her eyes are too bright. I know these danger signs but Hamish doesn't: he yaks on for ages, not realizing he's stepping into a minefield.

'Apart from damage to the roof, trees of this size are very bad for the foundations of an old house like this,' he says finally.

I feel a moment of sharp pity for him. He's taken such a lot of time and trouble over finding out what's wrong with the roof, and Mum is obviously cross and not at all appreciative.

'What nonsense,' she replies sharply. 'That's what Ralph-from-next-door is always saying. I don't know what it is with men and trees. They have only to see one and they want to cut it down. I abhor this preoccupation with making the world uniform and tidy. And as for saying that trees are bad for the foundations! It's absolute rubbish. This house is rock solid and the trees have been growing up against the sides of it for years. Apart from that—have you any idea how long it takes for a tree to reach full maturity? These trees are still babies. It would be a barbaric act to cut any of them down.'

Hamish stares at her for a moment and then he reaches forward and tries to hand the multi-coloured map over to her. At the same time he says something soothing about her having plenty of time to think it over and not to fret.

'I don't need to think anything over,' she says, pushing the map away and refusing to take it. 'I know I don't want any of the trees cut down. I'll have the other work done when I can afford it, but the trees must stay.'

I feel another moment of sympathy for him. I'm all soft-hearted today. But he has gone to such a lot of trouble with that map, and now Mum won't even look at it.

Hamish leans back in his chair and says nothing. He's looking a bit shell-shocked. When my mother digs her heels in she is like a mule—and it's always a nasty surprise to people who've come up against only her sweet, gentle side. It's obvious that Hamish can't handle her at all. Whereas I'm absolutely certain that Ralph would have been able to talk her round. He's got such a wonderful bedside manner—whereas Hamish is Mr Blunt. He tells it like it is—which is fine for poetry but not good for trying to get Mum to change anything in the house or garden. Like Auntie May she wants to keep it as a time capsule of a happier and gentler era.

Next day it starts pouring again—a really terrible storm that rolls around the city all morning and then moves out towards the North Sea. Within an hour it sweeps back over us again with renewed force: dark sea-water-laden clouds and thunder that sounds like bombs.

It's grim and there is no sign of Hamish. It's a shame

he's deserted us because we are once again running up and down stairs with buckets and mops. I find myself wishing he was here—because Broken Glass and Cara are both terrified of thunder and lightning and refuse to go up to the attic. Mum is trying to cook a Sunday roast and is really short-tempered, so it is left to me to try to stop the containers from overflowing.

The sound of the storm is deafening in the attic, the noise seems to get right under the eaves. It rolls around the dark spaces at the top of the roof magnifying and echoing as if the whole place is alive. It is spooky and I keep my nerve only by thinking about Ash and wondering if it's raining in Scotland and if he's having a good time. When I hear my phone I race down to my bedroom. I am sure that it's him ringing and by some magical thought-transference he knows that I need to speak to him NOW, this minute!

It's not him. It's Reece Browne. I swallow down my bitter disappointment and try my hardest to sound moderately friendly and not completely hacked off.

'I've just rung and managed to get hold of Ellen,' he says anxiously.

'Great, how is she?' I ask.

'I'm worried about her. She said she'd been ill with a stomach bug but is better now. She sounds really down.'

'Ellen hates being ill, that's all it is,' I say soothingly. 'She'll be all right. She'll be having a great time. You loved going on safari, didn't you? Ellen and her family were staying in a cool hotel out in the bush, and then having a week in Mombasa by the sea. It'll have been fantastic—the holiday of a lifetime,' I add, trying to keep envy out of my voice. Staying at home and looking after the cousins never seemed more tedious.

'Who are you trying to kid, Rose? You know she didn't want to go. She was dreading the flight and being in Africa. And I'm worried she's having a really crap time,' he says quietly.

I am really startled and shocked by this. I thought I was the only person Ellen confided in. She hasn't even confessed to Ash how much she hates flying and being away from home and foreign food. All the things the rest of us really enjoy.

'She had all kinds of potions and pills to take during the flight,' I say. 'Her mother got stuff from the health food shop and the doctor—so she'll have been fine. And there's your party to look forward to when she gets back so that'll make the return journey a breeze. She'll be fine if she has something else to focus on,' I say encouragingly. 'It's mind over matter.'

I have to make a big effort to be upbeat because I am really hurt that Ellen has told him so much personal stuff about herself. I suppose I will just have to accept that she really does want him for a friend—and that she talks to him like she talks to me.

But I don't want to talk to Reece. Although I can't find it in myself to be offhand—I owe him such a debt for the generous way he treated Cara, Crystal, and me. And I don't dislike him. In a way I can even understand why Ellen is fond of him—for a boy he's extraordinarily caring and gentle. I just don't want Ellen to like him more than she likes me.

'I must tell you,' he adds, when I try to get him off the phone. 'Ellen says to let you know that she's been on the Internet and seen your uncle on a web site: jexandthebaddies.www.usa. She says he's written a song using your mother's poem and it's really cool.'

'What?' I say. He repeats it all to me again, including the web address, as if I am really dim, whereas it's just that my head is reeling from what he has told me. 'My mother's poem—which one?' I ask bemused.

'Ellen said the one about the mermaid. Is everything all right, Rose? I haven't upset you, have I?'

'No . . . no, of course you haven't upset me. I've just got a bit of a cold,' I lie quickly. 'It's been really great to

hear from you, Reece. And thank you for the other day—
you were so kind to Cara. She hasn't stopped talking
about it. Look, when you next speak to Ellen give her
my love and tell her to ring me.'

'Yes, yes, I'll do that. I'm going to phone her again
tonight. And I don't care how long it takes or how much
it costs, I'm going to get through to her,' he says firmly.

'That's really kind of you. I'm sure that she'll appreciate
it,' I say stiffly. He's talking like a best friend—or a crush.
My heart sinks. Ellen seems hell bent on getting herself
into a muddle over this boy. I shall have to try to talk to
her about him when she gets home. But for the moment
I have other worries on my mind.

'Ring me and let me know how she is,' I say.

'I will, Rose. Bye.'

My instinctive reaction is to rush downstairs to find
my mother and blab. I want to tell her everything about
Milo and the poem and for her to make it all better. But
instead I sit down on my bed, take a deep breath and try
to visualize Ash and what he would say to me. He would
advise a scientific approach. Ash is big on science. He
says I rush into everything without collecting and
collating facts. Evidence . . . I need evidence . . . And I
need an aim, a method, and a conclusion, all that boring
stuff that makes scientists really good at getting at the
truth.

I sit for ages making a plan. Then I remember the marg
and ice cream containers in the attic and rush upstairs to
empty them into a bucket. It is while I am emptying the
bucket into the bath that I work out my first strategy.

After I have sorted the attic I brush my hair and calm
myself. Then I go downstairs to the kitchen.

'Can I do anything to help?' I say.

'Yes please,' Mum says distractedly. 'You could stir this
batter for me. It's for the Yorkshire puddings. I really
need to get them in. The meat is done, but the cooker
has gone cold. I suppose the gas pressure must be low

this morning. Or maybe the little gas jets in the oven need cleaning again. There's always such a lot to do,' she adds miserably.

I beat the mixture for a while and then stop for a breather. 'Mum. Did you ever write song lyrics?' I ask.

'No—not really . . . Why do you ask?' Mum says.

'It's just some of your poems would make good songs—wouldn't they?'

'Well, funnily enough, before I started writing poetry, when I was still at school, I used to help Milo with his lyrics. I would scribble ideas down and he would change them into songs. He used to say that we were a good team. He's very talented. Some people say he's a genius,' she says.

'Well, so are you,' I say defensively.

Mum laughs. 'Thank you, poppet. That's very kind of you, but I'm not in the same league as Milo. But I am very happy with my book of poems and it is a great thrill to be asked to read them at the Ilkley Literature Festival. I am looking forward to it. It will be my first public reading.'

'You sent your book to Milo—didn't you?' I say casually. I remember Mum sending off a pile of brown envelopes when her book came out. 'Did he like them?'

'Yes, I think he did,' Mum says, avoiding my eyes. 'I'm almost sure he phoned to congratulate me.'

'That's nice,' I say.

OK, I think to myself. First stage is fact finding. Milo has the poems and he has used Mum's work in the past. Next thing I need to do is to get on the Internet and see what is happening for myself.

I go in search of Broken Glass and Cara. They are glued to the TV watching cartoons.

'Is the Internet café open today?' I ask airily.

'No,' Crystal says, and her mouth closes like a trap after she has spoken. We don't ever say more to each other than we have to.

'Do you email your dad when you go there?' I ask in a chatty, conversational tone.

'Yes,' says Cara.

'No—we don't,' says Crystal. Then she turns fiercely to Cara and scowls.

'No—we don't,' Cara parrots obligingly. Sometimes I get really fed up with the way Cara pretends to be devoted to me but when the chips are down she sides with Broken Glass. I can only suppose that the bonds of sisterhood are stronger than I have realized. Either that or Crystal gives her a good slap if she steps out of line.

Anyway I know enough now.

But I am stuck. I need access to the Internet. Ash has it. Ellen has it. But they are both away. I could ring someone else from our class. But I am embarrassed. I don't know how to start to explain what I am doing. It all sounds a bit barmy.

I go back upstairs and sit on my bed wondering what to do. Then I phone Hamish. I know he has the Internet and he has proved himself to be kind and reliable. He is a poor substitute for Ash and Ralph but I need someone to help me. The other advantage with him is that I won't have to explain too much. He knows all about Mum's poems and quite a bit about Milo.

'I need to see you now, please,' I mumble down the phone. 'But not here. It's important. Somewhere in town maybe?'

'OK, meet you in Nelson's in fifteen minutes. We could have some lunch.'

I manage to suppress a groan. I haven't got any make-up on. My jeans are rather grubby and there is no time to change. I seem cursed. For years I have longed to lunch at Nelson's and now I am going there once again looking like a tramp.

'Thanks,' I say. 'And, Hamish, do me a favour, please don't say anything about this to my mother for the time being.'

When I get down to the kitchen Mum is absorbed in a book and there is a distinct smell of burning coming from the oven. I'd thought I was hungry but the smell of charred batter makes me feel quite sick.

'I'm just popping out for an hour. Amelia needs to see me to discuss our dance. Leave my dinner in the pantry; I'll heat it up when I get back,' I say, dropping a hasty kiss on my mother's cheek.

'Oh, darling,' she says, concerned. 'I've gone to such a lot of trouble, can't you stop and eat with us.'

'I think your puddings are ready,' I say as I make my escape. 'They smell a bit singed.'

Hamish is waiting outside Nelson's looking out for me and frowning anxiously. He hurries over to meet me: 'Rose, what is going on? You're not in some kind of trouble, are you?'

'No—it's not me—I need to talk to you about my mother's poems.'

His face clears. 'Come on then, ma bonny lassie. We'll have some lunch and you can tell me all about it.' He is so relieved he laughs as he says this.

I gulp and say, 'Thank you very much. But I don't think I can eat anything—I am all wound up inside.'

'Well, we'll see,' he says kindly.

He actually orders loads of scrummy stuff. Welsh rarebit with mixed salad and bacon and avocado wraps. 'Enough to share,' he tells the waitress. 'But for the moment we will just have a cold drink. Could you please bring the food in about fifteen minutes? Now, what is the problem?' he asks me.

I'd thought I was only going to tell him about the mermaid poem that Milo has used, but once I start everything that is troubling me comes flooding out: the poem, the hellishness of living with the cousins, the cheque that has never arrived, and finally the debt to Mrs Valente. I'm really stressed by the time I've finished. Hamish hands me a big clean hanky and looks away while I mop my face and blow my nose.

The waitress brings over our freshly squeezed orange juice and seeing my flushed, upset face gives Hamish a really nasty look and whispers to me, 'Are you all right, dear?'

I suddenly realize how bad it looks sitting here with him and nearly crying. 'Yes, thank you, I'm fine,' I gulp. 'Sorry,' I say to him. 'She obviously thinks you are the father from hell.'

Hamish smiles. 'I don't have a daughter but I do have two sons, so it doesn't bother me.'

'I didn't know you had children,' I say.

'They are grown-up now. Duncan is twenty-three and Bruce twenty-five.'

'That's old,' I say bluntly.

'I was married when I was in my teens and the boys were born soon afterwards. But my life changed a great deal when I was in my twenties. I was desperate to leave Glasgow and my old ways behind and sadly my wife and I grew apart. Education can bring people together but it can also divide them. But we are great friends still, and I'm very proud of my boys and I hope they are proud of me.'

'I expect they are. You've done very well, haven't you?'

He gives me a bit of a wry smile and says, 'Enough of me. Let's take your problems one by one. First, we will look on the Internet and see what is going on with Milo and the lyrics. Second, Milo will have to pay up the money he owes your mother for looking after the girls and for using her poem. And I will make sure he does. Which brings us to Mrs Valente's bill, which I think is concerning you very much, lassie?'

'Yes, it's bad enough having to put up with Br— I mean, Crystal, being so awful. But I hate going in to the Academy every day and rehearsing the show knowing there is no way we can pay for the costumes and practice clothes.'

'It must be bad if it's putting you off your food,' Hamish says kindly, and I nod. 'Do you have a middle name, Rose?' he asks. It seems a strange question but I answer.

'I was called Florence after Auntie May's baby sister who died in infancy. And I was named Rose because they were her favourite flowers. Auntie May is very important to my mother. That's why she's funny about the garden,' I explain.

Hamish nods, as if he understands. He is easy to be with. He doesn't talk unless he's got something important to say and I like that.

I watch while he takes a small notebook and pen from his pocket and begins to write. He has very old-fashioned loopy handwriting which is impossible to read upside down. He must know I am nearly dying with curiosity because eventually he passes the pad over to me and I read:

I, Rose Florence Asquith of The Anchorage, Sunderland Road, Durham, the undersigned, do promise to pay the following amount of money to Hamish Fergus MacCrimmon of No 3, Bexley House, Graves Crescent, Durham on receipt of the said amount arriving from Milo Asquith currently residing in the US of A, the father of Crystal and Cara Asquith. The said amount being monies owing to Mrs Valente of The Valente Academy, Durham. The said amount shall be paid out in a cheque payable to Mrs Valente and repaid to Hamish Fergus MacCrimmon in any suitable currency.

'Now how much is it in total that is owing?' he asks.

'You mean you will give me a cheque to give to Mrs Valente?' I say, stunned.

'Yes, and this document makes a legal agreement that I shall be paid when the money arrives from Milo.'

'But . . . Hamish . . . that's very kind of you. But what happens if he doesn't pay? It doesn't look likely that we'll ever get a penny out of him at the moment.'

Hamish smiles at me. It makes his eyes crinkle. He looks like Ash does sometimes when he is about to tell a joke. 'It just so happens that my publisher is in New York and he has been asking me for ages to pay him a visit. I think I shall call in on Milo while I am over there and get your money and an undertaking on what is happening at the end of the holidays.'

'I don't want the cousins to stay with us. Mum doesn't seem to mind—but I do,' I say bluntly.

He's surprisingly easy to tell the truth to. Maybe he should have been a psychiatrist instead of a poet.

'I know,' he says quietly. 'And it's only natural. You only have your mother. You don't want to share her with anyone. I'm sure that I'd feel the same in your situation.'

'Oh no!' I say quickly, because I don't want him to think I'm some jealous little kid. 'It's not like that at all. In fact—I'm quite keen to share my mother. It's not that I don't love her or anything. It's just—well—she really needs a partner her own age to hang out with, doesn't she? And I think it would be great if she had someone else to love, apart from me.'

He gives me a quizzical look. 'How very kind you are, Rose. How generous spirited.'

His praise embarrasses me a bit and maybe it's because of this that my mouth goes into gear before my brain starts to work. 'I've got great hopes that she'll marry our next-door neighbour, Ralph,' I say in a rush, and then I clamp my hand over my mouth in distress. 'Oh-my-goodness-I-can't-believe-I-just-said-that. I haven't told anyone else . . .' I say miserably. 'And I don't know why I've told you,' I add a bit accusingly. As if he might have elicited the information from me by devious means, which isn't the case at all.

'It's all right, lassie, don't fret,' he says, his Scottish voice soft and soothing. 'I'll not tell a soul. I'll take it to my grave, you have my word on it. Your mother is very lucky to have you taking such an inter-est in her future and well-being,' he adds rather sadly.

And I wonder if his sons don't bother with him too much.

'Come along, Rose, sign our agreement,' he says gently. 'Then we can have our lunch.'

I sign my name. He writes a cheque. I think it's a huge amount but he doesn't even blink. After he has handed me the cheque and I have thanked him profusely he waves the waitress over and she brings our food.

'I am starving!' I say with surprise.

Hamish manages a smile, although I think he still looks a bit miserable. Maybe he's thinking about his sons and wishing he had a daughter like me to look out for him. Poor old Hamish. I feel really fond of him today because he's been absolutely brilliant—a godsend—a complete hero.

'Good, I'm glad you're hungry. I hoped you might get your appetite back,' he says. 'And after lunch we'll collect your mother, go to my flat, and sort out the poem on the Internet. No more problems, Rose.'

'No more problems!' I echo as I tuck into the Welsh rarebit which is hot and tangy and utterly mouthwatering. Phoning Hamish has turned out to be a blinding choice. I feel happier than I have for weeks and weeks.

12

It's a drag that Crystal and Cara have to come with us to Hamish's flat. They don't seem keen and I would have loved to have left them at home. It seems ages since Mum and I did anything on our own. Also I am curious about Hamish's flat and I don't want Cara hanging around and asking questions. I like looking around other people's homes. I think you can tell a lot about people by how they live. I mean you have only to step into the coach house and see all that neatness to know that someone competent and in charge like Ralph lives there.

Hamish's flat is interesting. It's not very tidy, but not a tip either: it's crammed with books and fascinating old things and comfortable bits of furniture. Nicest of all he has two cats and a small dog. Cara's in seventh heaven because one of the cats likes to be picked up. So Cara wanders around with the moggy in her arms singing, 'Ding dong bell, pussy's in the well', and 'Hey diddle diddle, the cat and the fiddle.'

Broken Glass in contrast sits in a chair and scowls.

I play with the dog, a ginger mongrel called Badger, who likes to have his ears tickled and fetches his toys if you throw them.

Hamish has obviously told Mum what is going on because she is really stressed. She paces backwards and forwards while Hamish boots up his computer and goes online.

'Here we are,' Hamish says. He's arranged chairs around his desk so we can sit and see the screen. He's also made us tea and hot chocolate and provided gorgeous chocolate biscuits. He's been very kind. I give him a grateful smile.

'I haven't had a chance to look at the web site so I'm not sure how much there is,' he says. 'Are you all comfortable?'

We nod. He clicks the mouse and the web page opens. Milo is in the middle of a group of other musicians but I spot him straight away. His hair used to be curly like Mum's but now it is very short and his face is more lined and bony than I remember. The last few years of hardship seem to have taken their toll on him.

Jex, the leader of the band, is talking. (He's a bit of a laid-back old hippie and talks very slowly and deliberately as if he's started the day with a shot of bourbon.) He rabbits on for a while and then introduces Milo. He and all the other band members turn to look at Milo: he is their guest singer and they all say complimentary things about him and mention his classic songs from the Eighties.

Jex says that Milo is a song-writing genius and announces they are in rehearsal (as if we didn't know!) and will cut a new CD with the songs they are working on. I risk a glance at my mother. Her face is very set, as if she is in pain and fighting it. But she manages to turn to Crystal and Cara and attempt a smile: 'Isn't it lovely to see your father,' she says. They both look bored or fed up or both. Mum doesn't seem to have realized they have been down to the Internet café so have doubtless seen it all before.

The band starts to play their instruments and Milo begins to sing. As soon as he starts I can hear that it is Mum's poem, but not Mum's poem: half lines and images have been stolen from her work and put together differently.

'Ocean's widow
Horizon's child

Soft upon
Dreadlocked rocks
Where the sea
Is wild.
Oh, what secrets do you keep, sleeping in the conch-shell deep?'

he sings. It makes a good song. I have to admit that it sounds lovely. He's got the ebb and flow of the tide and the movement of the waves caught up in the music.

'Salty sister
Sea-lions' friend
Shrieking with
The circling gulls
At the dark
World's end.
Oh, what secrets do you keep, diving in the rolling deep?'

It finishes. Mum's face is very pale. Hamish stops the computer.

'He might have asked me,' she says wiping her eyes. 'I would have thought it over.' She gulps. 'I can't very well go and read my poems to people if they are going to turn on their radio and hear bits of them as songs, can I?'

'All you need to do is make him give you a credit on the CD cover and mention in passing that your poems have inspired your brother's lyrics. Your work came first and it stands alone,' Hamish says soothingly.

Mum nods a bit tearfully. 'Let's watch the rest of it. I wonder how many more he has used.'

I am aware of Crystal moving restlessly. 'I think Cara needs the loo,' she whispers to Mum, who isn't listening. Crystal grabs Cara's hand and makes a hasty exit.

Broken Glass is up to something. I just know she is. I've seen that sly look on her face before. I am torn between following them and watching the screen. The screen wins.

Milo is singing again: two, three more songs and all taken from Mum's work.

125

Mum is busy scribbling down notes and Hamish is watching and listening with a face like stone. Every so often he murmurs something to Mum that I can't quite catch.

Then Milo says, 'This is my latest song—work in progress,' and he laughs.

'Does it have a title?' someone asks.

Milo laughs again. 'Not yet. I just call it "Clockwork Heart".'

He sings the first line of the song, but I don't hear the rest because Mum gives a shriek as if a red-hot needle has been thrust into her heart. And then she and Hamish clutch at each other as if they are on board *Titanic* and the command to lower the lifeboats has just been made. Badger gives a startled bark and disappears under the sofa. I would like to do the same. Mum is going off like a mad woman. She's using words I didn't even know she knew. Swearing like a slapper and not at all like a respectable lady poet who teaches at a university.

'Mum!' I say shocked. 'It's not your poem, is it?'

Mum bursts into a storm of weeping and covers her face with her hands. 'How did he get it? How on earth did he get hold of it? I've been looking for it everywhere since it went missing. And I swear I never sent it to him. The bastard—the f—'

'Mum!' I shout so loudly that Badger gives a little howl of distress. He obviously thinks Hamish's visitors are busy murdering each other. 'Mum! What on earth is going on?'

Hamish turns to me. He has the strangest expression on his face. 'The poem is mine. I gave a copy of it to your mother.'

I turn away from them both. Mum is still weeping and Hamish has a protective arm around her shoulders and is crooning words as if she is a baby.

I listen to the song. And-oh-my-goodness-the-lyrics-are-absolutely-terrible! It's a love song. A really soppy mushy 'I looked up and saw your face and fell in love' type love song. The kind of crap that gets played on the radio on a Sunday morning that has you falling off your chair laughing or reaching for the sick bag.

'I'll love for all eternity
Remembering your smiles
I'll beat the seconds with my heart
In endless empty whiles
Until you're mine I count the days
Until you're mine I watch the clock
There is an old infinity
Between each tick and every tock.'

'You wrote that?' I say incredulously to Hamish.

I watch his jaw tighten. 'He's used it pretty much word for word. Do you think I should feel flattered?' he replies bitterly.

'How did he get it? Someone must have taken it out of my desk drawer. I never showed it to a soul,' Mum says beseechingly to him.

I don't like to say I should sincerely hope she hasn't shown it to anyone because they would wonder why she was bothering with such a load of old tripe. And as for Hamish—he should have consigned it to the waste-paper basket instead of showing it to my mother. Honestly, what a way to carry on.

'I suppose every poet has an off day,' I mutter to myself.

'How did he get it?' Mum laments.

The penny drops with all of us at the same moment.

'Crystal!' Mum and I say together.

'Of course,' Hamish says.

'But why?' I say.

'Let's ask her,' Mum says, and she leaps out of her seat and dashes off. There is a long moment of silence in the sitting room. I avoid Hamish's eyes.

'I'm sorry, wee Rosie,' he says; his accent is very broad.

'Don't apologize. There's nothing for you to be sorry about is there?' I say stiffly.

'Well, there is, and I am sorry about it,' he says again.

His smile is very rueful. Something tugs inside my heart at the sight of it.

'What on earth have you got to be sorry about?' I demand rather rudely.

'Och . . .' he says, shaking his head and turning away from me. 'I'm sorry that I'm not Ralph-from-next-door.'

'OH-MY-GOODNESS!' My voice is so horribly loud that poor little Badger whines in protest. 'You don't mean you . . . you and my mother. That you . . . that the poem . . .?'

'I wrote the poem because I am in love with your mother,' he says.

'But you hardly know her. You only met a few weeks ago!'

'I knew from the very first moment I saw her,' he says. 'But she values and loves you above everything and anyone in the world. And I'm not Ralph-from-next-door, am I?'

'No, nothing like him at all,' I say, and then as soon as I've said it realize how tactless it sounds. Poor Hamish—he's tried so hard to be helpful and he's been such a good friend to us all. 'I mean Mum and Ralph have known each other such a long time,' I say a bit desperately. 'Ralph and Ash have lived next door to us for three years and we're all so close and fond of each other. We're a bit like a family already. And Ralph is just right for my mother. I mean they go together like bread and cheese or eggs and bacon. You know—different but complementary.'

'Like your mother you have a wonderful way with words. I see perfectly what you mean,' Hamish says. And he smiles so bravely I almost feel like giving him a hug.

'Well, that's all right then,' I say consolingly.

Mum comes rushing into the room. 'Crystal is locked in the bathroom and refuses to come out. Cara is in floods of tears as well. I can't get a word of sense out of either of them.'

'Oh goodness, it's all my fault. I wanted them to come and stay and now everything is terrible,' I wail.

Hamish holds up his hands. 'Stop crying, both of you. It's no one's fault, no one is to blame. It doesn't even matter about the poem. I didn't ever expect or hope to publish it. It was a scribble—nothing more. I'm going to make a pot of tea and put poor Badger out in the garden for some peace and quiet. And then we will sit down and discuss this sensibly and calmly. Rose, please go and ask Crystal to come here and explain herself. Tell her there is absolutely no need for tears or tantrums. I don't think either Badger or I can cope with any more histrionics,' he adds firmly.

This speech calms Mum and me right down as if someone had used water cannon on us. Mum sits down on the sofa and starts to look normal again instead of a crazy person. I bite my lip and go and fetch Cara and Crystal. 'You've got to stop crying and making a fuss. Hamish is taking it very well. He's making us some tea. Now just chill out!' I snap. 'They just want the facts.'

It takes a bit of time to get the truth out of Crystal and she cries quite a lot and is pathetic. 'I didn't want to stay with you. I said as soon as it was mentioned that I would hate it and it would be awful. I wanted to go to America with Dad.' She snivels and Mum looks sad.

'I'm sorry you haven't enjoyed staying with us,' she says. 'Rose and I have tried very hard to make you welcome.'

Crystal shoots a glance at me. 'I've hated every minute of it,' she says dramatically.

'So tell us about the poem,' I say pointedly.

'Dad promised me that if the recording went well he would send for us. He promised we could join him.' Crystal's voice rises with desperation. 'But then he said he was stuck because he didn't have enough material and it was slowing everything down.' She wipes her eyes and continues. 'I was really upset when he said there was no chance. But I knew he was using the book of poems that Auntie Hal had written so I looked on her desk for some more. I thought it would solve the problem. And I really didn't think one more would make any difference. You've got hundreds of them, haven't you? Your desk is covered with them,' she says to Mum. 'So I had a good look around and I sent that one because it was so nicely typed. It didn't have any name on it. It could have been the binman's for all I knew,' Crystal finishes, a bit sulkily.

'Crystal, dear, I don't think your father will ever send for you to go to America, even if you send him hundreds of poems,' Mum says quietly. 'I do understand what was going through your head and I forgive you. But you must understand that you have to stay with us, until either your mother or father return to this country. You must stop hoping for the impossible and accept that is the situation and none of us can alter it.'

'But I hate it here. And I hate the dancing show. And I hate Rose!' Crystal bursts out. 'She calls me Broken Glass!'

A hot blush of shame and embarrassment covers my face and neck. 'You call me Thorn,' I say lamely. But I do feel bad. She's years younger than me and she's staying in my home. It makes me look like some kind of awful bully.

To my surprise Hamish bursts out laughing. 'Oh, hush now, child,' he says to Crystal. 'I think in the great scheme of things a few names aren't going to hurt you. Rose has gone to a great deal of trouble on your behalf. Be grateful for that and stop whining. I'm sure you are more than capable of giving as good as you get. We have a very rude name for children like you in Glasgow—which I shall not repeat—but believe me it makes Broken Glass seem like a real compliment.'

The thought of this rude name makes him chuckle. 'Have a chocolate biscuit and stop blubbing,' he adds to her. 'Just remember that I am the injured party here, not you.'

Crystal gives him a dark look and mops her eyes. I would like to say thanks to him for sticking up for me but I am embarrassed. I owe him quite a lot in one way and another. The debt to Mrs Valente cleared, Crystal put in her place, the promise of making Milo pay up. I wonder if he has done it all because he is sweet on Mum. I feel a bit sorry for him over that as well. I mean there is just no competition between him and Ralph. Ralph is everything that Mum could possibly want: plus the fact that he is younger and better looking and has a blameless past. I have sometimes worried about Ralph's lack of interest in poetry. Sharing interests can be important in a relationship. But I honestly don't think it matters now I have seen Hamish's attempt at romantic verse. Poor old Hamish has proved a duffer on that front as well. Goodness only knows what Mum made of that soppy poem. It was the kind of thing you find in birthday cards, and is miles worse than some of the terrible stuff Mum's undergrad students churn out.

Hamish is telling us about his trip to America. 'I have already arranged to call in to see Milo, and it will be an amicable and friendly visit,' he adds when he sees Crystal's agitation on hearing this news. 'I don't intend to fall out with anyone over a few lines of verse. But I am keen he should give acknowledgements and payment for material used and for money owing,' he adds with a glance at me. We both know to what he is referring and I give him a grateful smile.

I am brimful of emotion by the time we get home. To my enormous relief Ash phones and I tell him everything: all my plans for Ralph and my mother, the problems with Milo and Crystal, and last of all the news about Hamish and the love poem and Hamish's hopeless feelings for my mother. Ash doesn't say anything at all. I am disappointed.

'We are coming home tomorrow early. I will talk to you then,' he says. He sounds tired and grumpy.

'Just tell me what you think,' I say. I feel as high as a kite. 'I can't wait until tomorrow,' I add urgently.

'OK then, Rose, if you really want to know. I think you should stop meddling in other people's lives. It's completely out of order,' he says. 'You've bullied Ellen about Reece. You've told Hamish a load of stuff that is all in your head. What proof have you got that my father and your mother are attracted at all? I would have said they are at best indifferent and at worst actually dislike each other. Them getting married is a totally crap idea. You must be a bloody lunatic to have thought of it in the first place.'

'Your father is very fond of my mother,' I say stung. 'He always makes a real fuss of her.'

'Fond of her? I don't think so. He refers to her as "That-dizzy-blonde-next-door" and "Halcyon-Air-Head".'

'He never does!'

'My father is very kind to people who are ill, supremely compassionate to people who are dying, and rather harsh on the rest of us. If your mother needed a Caesarean section she would be of some interest to him. Other than that—zilch. I'm afraid that in his view letting your house fall down around your ears is almost a criminal act. And he thinks your mother should be forced to tidy up her garden. He says it lowers the tone of the neighbourhood. You may think he's some kind of superman, but you want to try living with him. He's hard on people. Very hard. Especially people like your mother.'

'You bloody shit. You're making it up!' I shout.

'Rose. I just want you to see things for what they are. Why don't you open your eyes? You get all these half-baked ideas in your head. Fancying Joshua-bloody-Browne and interfering with Ellen and Reece and now arranging your mother's life. And you can't see they are all fantasies. You can't see the truth when it's staring you in the face.'

'Oh shut up!' I scream. And I switch my phone off.

13

I am in a real stress. I am so upset I can't cry. I pace the floor of my room, backwards and forwards. I can't eat. When Mum calls me down for supper I make a hurried excuse and tell her to leave my food in the pantry and I will have it later. Her kindly enquiries drive me into the bathroom.

I run a bath and tip half a bottle of aromatherapy bath oil in. The bath oil was a present from Ellen. She's really interested in essential oils and always says lavender is very soothing. But it doesn't do anything for me. And the thought of Ellen: sweet, kind, gentle Ellen, makes me feel even worse. Have I really bullied her about Reece? I was only trying to help.

At least I can think about Ellen. My mind blanks out when I try to focus on Ash. I feel so ill at the memory of his words that I get out of the bath and stand over the basin expecting to start retching at any moment. Then, shivering and dejected and slippery, I get back into the water and soap my face, waiting for the release of tears. But they don't come. The sickness is deep in my heart, flooding through my veins, making me feel wretched. And I know then, with a rush of shame, that it is a sickness of the soul not of the stomach.

With a surge of emotion I know that I value Ash's good opinion more than anything in the world. I want so much for him to admire and respect me as I admire and respect him. He is the cleverest and the kindest person I know.

Thinking back over the years I have known him I

realize he has never said a bad word about someone if he could say something good, or done anything mean or dishonest. He is fair and kind and knowledgeable. If I had talked to him about all this at the beginning I would never have got into such a muddle. And now he will never want anything more to do with me. He thinks I am a stupid little kid—a 'bloody lunatic'.

His harsh words are burnt into my brain and I can't deny the truth of any of them. He has opened my eyes. I have been so unbelievably foolish. I saw in Ralph what I wanted to see—not what was there. Now I know him for what he is: a frail human being like the rest of us, riddled with faults and weaknesses. I thought he was some kind of god creature—the perfect father, a paragon of virtue—when in fact he is a bit of a narrow-minded control-freak who values a tidy garden above anything else.

Ralph is the complete antithesis of my mother. How on earth did I ever think they would get on together? I imagine Ralph trying to de-junk my mother's home and life and get her 'tidied up'—and I shudder at the thought. She'd probably never write another poem for the rest of her life.

Ash will think me the biggest fool in the world for even thinking about them getting together. And I told him everything—all about how I'd warned Hamish off. And for all I know my mother might be in love with Hamish—and I have messed up that along with everything else.

Mum and Hamish I can sort out. I will do a bit of match-making and get them together. But there is no chance of getting Ash's good opinion back. He will never trust me or like me again and I don't know how I can bear the pain of that.

'Oh-my-goodness-you-bloody-fool!' I say out loud to myself as I am washing my hair. The shampoo goes in my eyes and makes them water. I will pretend I am crying.

I should cry. I am such an idiot! What am I thinking of? 'Match-making' . . . I can imagine what Ash would say if he knew I was thinking of interfering with Mum and Hamish. Will I never learn to be sensible and not to meddle? Not if I don't have him for a friend I won't. No one else tells me the truth like he does. No one else sees me so clearly for what I am.

And up until now he has always been my biggest fan, my greatest supporter. He's always told me the truth, harshly sometimes, but he has always been on my side. I've always known I could rely on him and trust him. That he would put my best interests in front of everything else. That he cared for me and looked out for me at all times.

Painfully I realize what I have done. I have lost the best friend in the world. I cry then, proper tears. I thought it would be a relief but it isn't. I have thrown away something so precious I feel as if I will never recover. From now on I will go through life as half a person. And all the best bits of me, the bits that made me a really good person, are lost in that missing half. Truly, I will be the sound of one hand clapping.

I can't eat. I put my supper in the bin when Mum isn't looking. And I can't sleep. I lie awake through the long hours, listening to the sounds of the night: tree branches knocking on the windows and roof, a cat yowling, the far off hum of traffic, and the eerie hooting of an owl. When the birds begin the dawn chorus I doze off for a few moments, but when I hear a car pulling up at the back of the house, I jackknife out of bed.

The morning is dank and chilly. I pull on my fleece and race down the stairs. Greyish light is streaming in through the stained-glass skylight. I sit on the stairs and peer through the pink pane.

Ash and Ralph are unpacking their car, moving stealthily like burglars. The light snaps on in their kitchen. I see Ralph running the tap, filling the kettle, and the outline of Ash's broad shoulders in the background. Then Ash is at the window, looking out through the gloomy dawn, staring up at the skylight window, seeming for all the world to be looking straight into my eyes.

I draw back from the window with a little start of surprise, my hand over my mouth, my heart racing. When I dare to look out again they are sitting at the table eating breakfast. They are back to their calm well-ordered existence. I watch them, drawing comfort from the sight of Ash's face, his familiar russet hair, his wide smile. He laughs at something Ralph says. He looks fine. Falling out with me hasn't devastated his life in the way it has mine. I try to find it in my heart to be angry that he is happy and I am not. But I can't. He is blameless. I am at fault. It's as simple as that.

I console myself with the thought that I can at least see him even if we aren't speaking. I will come here later and watch again. But for now my hands are freezing and I am cold and cramped. I rise to my feet like an old woman, stretching my arms above my head. Out of the corner of my eye I see the door to Cara and Crystal's room close. It makes me feel uncomfortable to know that one of them has been up and about and might have seen me sitting on the stairs. I tell myself it was Cara going to the loo, too sleepy to notice me. Just as long as it wasn't Broken Glass spying—I shudder at the thought.

I get back into bed but I dare not close my eyes in case I oversleep. It's rehearsals at nine sharp. For the first time in my life I really don't want to go. My head is thudding. Eventually I get up.

Mum is in the kitchen, the oven is on with the door open, and I gravitate to its warmth. 'Mum, do you think you could please keep an eye on Crystal and Cara this week and bring them down for their rehearsal calls?' I ask. 'I'm sorry,' I add. 'I know I said I would look after them all the time while they are here. But it's such a drag trying to get them up and ready to leave with me first thing. And I'm going to be stuck at the Academy all day.' I try not to sound too miserable about this. 'And it's so boring for them to be hanging around.'

'Oh, poppet, of course I don't mind. You've been so very good about looking after them. I will walk down with them. It will do me good. I've been spending too much time at my desk. If it's a reasonable day I shall do some gardening. It's looking a bit of a shambles out there, isn't it? I might cut the grass if I can get the mower going.'

'Maybe Hamish will help?' I ask tentatively.

'He's off to the States sometime soon,' Mum says. 'He's very busy . . . And I think I've taken up enough of his time already. Anyway, we don't see eye to eye about the garden . . . do we?' She smiles ruefully.

'Mum, he is right about cutting down the trees,' I say.

'Do you think so?' Mum asks with astonishment.

'Yes,' I say firmly. 'And I think you should listen to what he says. I think he gives good advice.'

'About the garden?'

'About everything,' I say.

'I see,' Mum says quietly. 'I thought you felt like me about the garden.'

'Mum—everything in life has to change; it's the nature of things, isn't it? We can't hold on to the past.'

'No, maybe you're right,' Mum says, but she doesn't sound very certain.

'I shall have to get a move on,' I say, reaching for my file and looking at the rota. 'Cara and Crystal have a rehearsal call at 10 o'clock and then we all have a run through at 2 o'clock. After that it's a special rehearsal for the soloists which they can watch.'

I force down some toast and a cup of tea because I know I will need energy for the coming day. 'I'll get off to rehearsals,' I say to Mum, with an attempt at cheerfulness.

As I climb the stairs I feel a cold little wind tugging

at my bare feet and look around startled. Then I see the glistening of tiny shards of broken glass, shining like diamonds on the faded brown of the stair carpet. I look up at the skylight. The pink pane has been pushed out and broken. And through the gaping hole I can see the cold grey morning sky.

I make some kind of noise because Mum comes to the bottom of the stairs and asks me what is wrong.

'The window is broken,' I say.

'Oh damn,' Mum grumbles. 'Not another job that needs doing? Is there broken glass on the carpet? Don't walk on it in your bare feet, darling.'

She brings a dustpan and brush. 'I'll put some tape over it. It's only one little pane that has gone. How strange. I hope a bird didn't fly into it,' she says.

I don't reply. I go upstairs and get showered and dressed in my rehearsal clothes. When I walk downstairs I see ugly black masking tape covering the place where the pink glass used to be. It's impossible to see through any of the other panes—the colours are too dark. I have lost my little window on the world. I have lost my view of Ash. My heart is heavy.

'You look terrible,' Amelia says bluntly to me when I get to the Academy. 'Are you ill?'

'No—just tired,' I say.

'Well, if you're tired now you'll be dead by the end of the day. Mrs Valente has got 'em packed in like sardines, and here come the first lot.'

Rehearsals are getting really hectic. I have a group of babies who have never been on stage before. I have started preparing them for what it will be like. Every rehearsal I go through the whole routine: how they must go to the loo before getting into their costumes and hold hands in the wings. I prepare them for waiting in darkness, and, most important of all, teach them how not to fall off the edge of the stage.

'God, you're wonderful with them,' Amelia whispers,

as we play the 'closing our eyes and waiting for the music' game for the fourth time. 'They're driving me nuts.'

I smile and shake my head. It's good to be busy. It takes my mind off my troubles.

Crystal and Cara arrive. 'We asked Auntie Hal if we could stay and watch you and Amelia rehearse this afternoon,' Cara says, and my heart sinks. I feel ghastly. The last thing I need is Crystal watching me dance.

'Well, you won't have to make any noise,' I say a bit snappily, and Cara looks hurt. Crystal gives me a glance from under her dark lashes and I see a trace of a smile. She's rattled me and she knows it. I shall have to keep my cool.

The rehearsal goes surprisingly well. We get through without a hitch. The Academy empties of students. 'Fifteen minutes, girls,' Mrs Valente says. She disappears off to the kitchen for a black coffee.

'I'm going to slip out for a doughnut for us,' Amelia says. 'I shall die if I don't have some carb before we do our dance.'

'Get me three jammies, please,' I say, handing over some change.

'Three!' Amelia squawks in horror.

I nod at Crystal and Cara and Amelia smiles with understanding. 'Are they watching us again? You'd think they'd be bored by now.'

'I'll tidy the cloakroom and make us a cup of tea while you're out,' I say to Amelia's retreating back. When Amelia wants a doughnut she really shifts.

I have time to pick up only two forgotten skirts from the floor before Amelia reappears. Her face is sheet-white, and she is holding her left arm against her body and panting slightly.

'Oh-my-God! Rosie! I slipped down the steps and took such a tumble. I think I've sprained my wrist. It really hurts . . .'

The whole of her begins to wobble and I shout to

Crystal for help as I leap across to Amelia and get her into a chair. 'Put your head down to your knees,' I say urgently. 'I think you're going to faint.'

'No I'm not, I'm fine now. I'm sorry, Rosie. My mother always said doughnuts would be my downfall and she was right . . .' Amelia is sobbing now. 'I can't dance the Beast with a sprained wrist, can I? Oh, how could I be so stupid?'

'Don't cry. It might be all right. It might just be bruised. Let me get Mrs Valente to have a look.'

Amelia's wrist is swollen and painful. Mrs Valente says it must be X-rayed and rings Amelia's mother. Crystal, Cara, and I stand in a dejected trio while Amelia is carted off to Accident and Emergency. Even if it's only a sprain it's going to be a sling job. Amelia is out of the show.

'Oh dear, poor, poor Amelia,' Mrs Valente says when Amelia has gone. 'And poor Rose, too. You've worked so hard on your dance. And I'm afraid it's far too late to rehearse someone else in the part. We'll have to do it next year,' she says consolingly.

'Crystal knows the Beauty dance,' Cara says, her voice very loud and clear. 'She dances in our bedroom before we go to sleep. I have to be the Beast. I stand and growl and she is frightened of me. And I hold her hand when she does the arabesque and she whispers she loves me. We play being Beauty and the Beast every night.'

'That's nice,' I say automatically.

Mrs Valente smiles absentmindedly and says, 'I shall have to change the running order. The second half will be much too short without your finale. Maybe we can move the *Animal Farm* scene . . .' She is reaching for her folder, absorbed in worry.

Cara interrupts again, ignoring my warning frown. She is tugging at my hand. 'Crystal dances nearly as nice as you, Rosie. She's really good as Beauty. She can't wear pointy shoes but she . . .'

'Do be quiet,' I hiss. I glance across at Crystal. She is

curling up in one of the chairs, hiding behind her curtain of hair, as if she would like to disappear.

'Do you really know the role of Beauty, Crystal?' Mrs Valente asks with surprise. 'You've watched every rehearsal, haven't you? But have you really learnt the steps?'

'Watch her! Watch her!' Cara shouts. 'She's really good.'

Mrs Valente gives me a questioning look and I shrug.

'Well, there's no one else who knows the role and you do have potential,' Mrs Valente says quietly. But Crystal still refuses to look up or speak.

'Crystal,' Mrs Valente's voice is firm. 'Please don't waste our time. I'm asking you a question. Do you think you might have learnt the steps to the dance while you were watching, or not? This is very important. Whatever disagreements you and Rose have had in the past must be forgotten. The show is very important to all of us. We need a replacement. Might you be able to stand in?'

'Yes,' Crystal mutters. 'But I've only learnt the Beauty part. I don't know the Beast . . . I don't like boy dancing.'

'I've learnt all of Amelia's steps. I know the Beast part,' I say quietly.

'Of course you have,' Mrs Valente says, smiling at me. 'Shall we try it? With you dancing the Beast? Crystal will have to dance on demi-pointe and you might have to improvise at times. But we might be able to cobble something together. What do you say, girls—shall we give it a try?'

Crystal says yes before I do. I think about all the things she's done that have made me hate her: breaking the window, stealing Hamish's poem from my mother's desk, watching me and Ash through the kitchen window and taunting me about him. I think about how she tried to humiliate me in front of Hamish and how awful it will be if she and Cara have to live with us after the end of the holidays. And I want to say 'NO' so much that my throat is tight. I can hardly bear to look at her, let alone dance with her. If she dances Beauty and I am the Beast I shall have to hold her waist in the pas de deux and kiss her hand. The idea makes me shudder. I couldn't be more repelled by her if she was a stag-beetle or a particularly horrid hairy-legged spider.

'Rose, dear.' Mrs Valente's voice is rather anxious. 'I don't want to pressurize you. Do you feel happy to take on the role of the Beast and dance with Crystal?'

I think about Ash. I think about what he would do in a situation like this. He would do the right thing. He would know that the show must go on.

'Yes, of course I'm happy about it. It's absolutely marvellous. What a piece of luck that we can swap roles. It's fantastic that Crystal has learnt my part,' I say swiftly, glibly, lying through my teeth. 'Crystal and I can practise at home together, can't we?' I add encouragingly. So great is our antipathy that normally we are never in the same room at the same time, so this will be an event in itself.

'Good girls,' Mrs Valente says encouragingly. 'Thank you so much for giving this a try. It might save the day. We'll leave the running order as it is for the time being. Come along. We'll go and have a run through and see how you cope.'

We are swept into the studio on the tide of her enthusiasm. My tiredness has reached the stage where I feel light-headed. I change into footless tights and stand in the middle of the studio, arms outstretched, listening to the overture; feeling the cool wood floor under my bare feet and the familiar exhilarating rush of emotion I get when waiting for a cue.

Crystal is standing facing me; her feet in fifth position, her hands clasped together. She is nervous, I can sense it. She looks across to me and her dark eyes meet mine. I think it's the first time she has ever looked at me frankly and openly without a sneer on her face. 'Thanks, Rose,' she whispers. She blinks and looks away quickly. Then our music begins and we dance.

14

I am a very tired and lack-lustre Beast and Crystal is a very nervous Beauty. But even so we are pretty amazing. 'What a wonderful rapport you two girls have,' Mrs Valente says with a sigh, because we have managed to get through the dance with only a couple of fluffs. 'And there was me thinking you didn't get on. You dance together as if you are totally in tune. Work at home and you will be magnificent. You have saved the show and you will be the stars, thank you.'

If I wasn't so exhausted, and so emotionally wrung out about Ash, I might find it in my heart to be jealous of Crystal. She has turned out to be a surprisingly good dancer. Even performing the part of Beauty on demi-pointe she is light and fluid. As soon as the music begins sulky Crystal disappears and Beauty emerges. It is magical to watch—all the bones and awkward edges of her body seem to disappear and she transforms into a creature of flowing lines. My one consolation is that she would be crap as the Beast. Boy dancing is definitely not her scene.

We don't talk on the way home. I keep waiting for my phone to ring. I keep thinking that surely Ash will get in touch. In the past whenever we've had a disagreement he's always been the first to send a text message. 'Soz.' And we've laughed and made up. But this time it's serious and there is nothing but silence.

There is no sign of Ralph's car. No sign of any activity in the coach house. I hang around in the kitchen for as long as I dare after supper hoping for sight or sound of him. There is no credit on my phone and I have no money left in my kitty so I can't ring him.

I count up the days until Reece's party when I am sure to see him. No one in their right mind would pass up an evening at Monty's. It's a really cool club and very strict about ID so we never normally get a chance to go there. Monty's parties are infamous and wild and talked about at school in hushed whispers. Ash is sure to go along because he will want to support Ellen, even if he isn't talking to me. So I console myself with the thought that I am bound to see him there. And surely it will be easier to make up when we are face to face?

But, before I have any chance of seeing him, we have two full days of rehearsals, a technical rehearsal, a dress rehearsal, and then the show. I have lots to do. I have babies who should be in nappies, stroppy nine year olds who have too many costume changes, and lots of mothers to organize. Mrs Valente relies on Amelia and me to help her. In the past it hasn't felt like a chore. I have revelled in my role of best helper. But now I don't think I want to be bossy and in charge. I want to be Ash's best friend. I can't seem to concentrate on anything else.

I get through it. Rehearsals are like being thrown into the deep end of the swimming pool when you are a non-swimmer. You learn fast how to do froggy-stroke because it's either that or drowning. So it is with the show. I force myself to think and care about it. Sometimes at odd moments the memory of Ash's silence comes back to haunt me and I feel a tightness in my throat. But I make myself think about the party on Saturday night. When we see each other it will be different. It must be . . .

Ellen, bless her, comes to help during the dress rehearsal and brings her video recorder. She's got awful jet lag but it's wonderful to have another pair of hands. I give Cara to her to be looked after. Cara is on cloud nine because she has the most quick-changes of any child in the entire show. She has to have Ellen as her very own dresser waiting ready in the wings to rip one costume off and replace it with another. And glory of glories, we find that at the start of the show she will have to wear three pairs of tights one on top of the other because there isn't time to change them. Cara boasts about this for ages. She is well on the way to being a superstar!

Crystal and I spend every spare minute working on our dance. It's funny: we still aren't friends—we are civil, that's all—but when we dance together it is as if we both become different creatures and lose sight completely of Thorn and Broken Glass. As soon as the music starts I become the Beast—tortured and passionate—and she tender, loving Beauty. I am grateful to be dancing the Beast. He is in such pain! It's a great way to get rid of some of the anger and emotions that are racing around inside my head.

During our tea break I ask Ellen, 'Have you heard from Ash? Is he dressing up for the party?' And I add quickly, 'I've only been at home to sleep for the last week.' Because I don't want her to know that Ash and I aren't speaking.

'He says he's going as a scruff. He says anything else is soppy. I said I could make him into one of the Blues Brothers with some of my dad's sunglasses, a shirt, and a tie but he just laughed. We're all coming to your show tomorrow afternoon so you'll see him then.'

'All?'

'Yes, Reece and me, Jessica and Ash and Josh—we've all got tickets. I thought we might go for a pizza afterwards.'

'Oh, how cosy,' I say glibly. I should be pleased they are all coming to watch the show. We have a huge theatre to fill and we've all been selling as many tickets as possible. So it's great that five of them are taking time out to come and watch my dancing school.

The trouble is it sounds like couples: Reece and Ellen, love's young dream, Ash and Jessica, and me and Joshua.

I don't know why I am so upset at that thought. 'I thought you'd be pleased,' Ellen says with satisfaction. 'Even though you say you don't like Josh any more I think you're still a bit keen on him.'

'I don't know, really,' I say weakly. I can't confess to Ellen that although Josh is just about the most fanciable boy I have ever met, and I have spent hours fantasizing about him in the past, I don't *like* him very much. Neither can I confess—because it's just so Junior School—that I am irrationally jealous of Ash and Jessica being bracketed together. I want to talk to Ash so much I simply cannot stand the idea of anyone else being with him—especially Jessica. It seems all wrong. I don't understand myself at all at the moment. Falling out with Ash seems to have turned my brain to mush. I can't think straight.

After the dress rehearsal Mum collects Crystal and Cara but Amelia and I stay and try to help Mrs Valente sort out lighting problems and a CD player that is on the blink. Amelia is still useful even with only one hand working. At nine o'clock I finally ring Mum to tell her I am on my way back and, to my surprise, when I leave the hall I find Hamish waiting for me.

'Thought you might like a lift after such a long day,' he says.

'Thanks,' I say gratefully. 'I'll just tell Amelia I don't need a ride.' Amelia's mother normally takes me home when we are late but they live in the opposite direction to us and I always feel like a bit of a burden. So it is lovely to have someone waiting especially for me. 'Do any of your friends need taking anywhere? I don't mind being a taxi,' Hamish says.

'They're all OK, but it's very kind of you.'

'I've ordered a pizza, thought you might like supper. It should be ready any minute now.'

'You angel!' I say happily. I normally have toast when I get home late but pizza is much better. 'How was America? Did you manage to see Milo?' I add a bit anxiously. I am still aware that I owe him a huge amount of money for the costumes and practice clothes. The burden of debt has moved from Mrs Valente to him and I still worry about it.

'I saw a great deal of your uncle Milo. We had some long and very profitable meetings and drank a great deal of Scotch and I still have the headache to prove it,' Hamish laughs. 'Please wipe that worried frown off your face, wee Rosie. I have all the money that is owing to your mother. It is in a banker's order and strictly above board and watertight.'

'And what about the money he owes you, the cheque for Mrs Valente that you paid?'

'That will come in time. Milo and I are now business partners. I deal with the money and he deals with the fame. An Englishman and a Scotsman together make a perfect combination. No one will rip him off with me as his financial adviser.'

He collects the pizza and puts it on my lap. 'We'll hurry you home and you can have it while it's hot,' he says. 'I got an Italian salad too.'

'Thanks very much,' I say. It is nice to be fussed over. 'So how come you and Milo are partners now?' I ask. I am wide-eyed with curiosity.

'Milo needs me,' Hamish says. 'Most partnerships are based on need.'

'But do you need him?'

Hamish laughs. 'Well, maybe I do.'

'So—tell me how it works,' I demand.

'I don't like flying. I'll confess that to you, Rosie. And I normally read a long classic novel when I have to cross the Atlantic.'

I try not to sigh because I don't want to hear about Hamish's phobias. I want to know what happened with Milo. 'Yes,' I say a bit pointedly and Hamish smiles.

'Well, this time I didn't read. I sat down with a notebook. I wrote down every single thing that came into my head. Daft stuff—anything at all—a stream of consciousness. It was like the thoughts that drift into your head just before you go to sleep: half-remembered memories that are sometimes clear and bright and other times as faded as a dream. I thought about the girls I liked when I was at school. I remembered fishing trips on Loch Erin when I was a boy. I recalled going to a jumble sale with my mother and the smell of second-hand clothes. Memories. Visions. Dreams. I didn't write anything about my life now: my lecturing, my home and friends, my books, my moggies and Badger. I'm not prepared to discuss the here and now or my hopes for the future. But my past—well, it is a bit of a rag and bone shop—and Milo and the world may have it with pleasure.'

'Why would Milo want your past?' I ask. I'm not keeping up with this at all.

'Because Milo has difficulty writing lyrics and, having studied his work, I know that in the past he relied on your mother more than he ever let on. His early songs were influenced largely by her. She used to write poems, short stories, and half-finished novels when she was at school and he plundered all of them for ideas and images. But he can't have her poetry now. It's too important to her. So I helped him out. Milo's next CD will be called "The Transatlantic Notebook" and will be credited to Milo Asquith, Jock, and Mary.'

'Who are Jock and Mary?'

Hamish laughs. 'Why, your mother and me, of course! Those are our pen names for song writing.'

'They sound like his dogs,' I say.

Hamish laughs. 'That doesn't matter as long as our names are credited on the CD and we are on the contract.'

'Does that mean you'll both get half the money?'

'Not half—just a small proportion of the royalties—but it will be a tidy wee sum for you and your mother. What is more important is that I have insisted that Milo has a lawyer and an agent to look after all our business interests. So there are safeguards in place to stop him blowing his share. My publisher was most helpful in arranging it all for me. No one will be able to rip Milo off ever again.'

'Have they in the past?'

'I suspect they might have. By rights he should be comfortably off and he's got nothing but debts to show for his early success. He admits he's not good with money and is generous to the point of madness. Very different to a canny Scot.' Hamish smiles.

'Thank the lord for a canny Scot!' I say with a sigh. 'Hamish! Can I tell you I think you're fantastic?'

'Och. It was nothing. Only a few scribbles and a wee bit of organizing,' he says. He seems embarrassed by my praise. 'I don't like to interfere in other people's lives but sometimes it is necessary. But I'm not going to make a habit of it,' he adds.

'Really you've done it to help my mother, haven't you?' I ask, swallowing hard and looking out of the car window so I don't have to see his face when he answers.

'Yes, and for you, lassie,' he says.

'Thanks,' I mutter. I am actually so choked up by what he has said that I can't say any more.

When we get back to the house there is a riot going on. 'We're going to Disneyland,' shouts Cara. Crystal is whirling around and smiling. SMILING! It's a rare and wonderful sight.

'Dad has just signed a contract with a new record label. A solo album. Mum's coming to fetch us and we are off to America for a holiday.' Crystal can't hide the glee on her face as she tells me this.

'Great!' I say. 'When is your mum coming?'

'Day after tomorrow,' Crystal says.

'Well, this is wonderful,' I say. My eyes meet Hamish's amused glance and I smile. 'What a surprise!'

'Yes, it is, isn't it?' Crystal says. 'And Dad has agreed

149

to put half the money he's going to earn into Mum's name so he can't spend it all. Mum says it's a miracle.'

'It certainly seems like it,' I agree. I tell myself that I do not mind that they are going away on a dream holiday and I am left at home. They've had a dreadful life: being dumped here with us, moonlighting from flats, their mother having to go away to work. Whereas I have a perfect life: my mother is always here for me, I never go without anything, and I have Ash living next door and Ellen for a best friend. I tell myself that to be even a tiny bit jealous of their trip to Disneyland is totally pathetic.

It won't go away though: a wormy jealous thought keeps sliding into my head, even when I am in bed and going through the steps of the Beast solo, still it slithers into my consciousness. 'It isn't fair,' a little voice laments. 'They are going to Disneyland—America—a proper holiday. And I am left at home. It isn't fair. It isn't fair.'

I kill it off. I ask myself which I would choose if I had the chance. Ash back as my best friend or a trip to Disneyland—and there is no competition. I would choose Ash. That is all I really want in the world. Tomorrow is the show, and after the show I will see him. He will be in the audience to see me dance the Beast. My stomach ties in a knot of tension and I feel a flutter run through my limbs. I don't know which is going to make me more nervous—dancing a solo that I have had only three days to prepare or seeing Ash. Sleep overtakes me before I can decide.

15

Getting up in the morning and getting ready for the show with Cara and Crystal is like a dream come true. We are all excited and happy, getting on together like sisters. We queue for the bathroom and make jokes, and then we sit around the kitchen table with mugs of hot chocolate and talk about how nervous we are. It just proves that dreams can and do come true, but not always in the way you expect them to.

When Crystal and I are alone in the kitchen I ask curiously, 'Why didn't you want to do anything when we first started rehearsals? You're a great dancer. You could have been in some good numbers instead of back row of the can-can and a couple of walk-on parts.'

Crystal shrugs. 'I stopped dancing when Mum went away. I was really angry and upset with her for leaving us. I mean, I know they needed the money and everything, but it was awful her going off like that. I kept on thinking she might not come back. I knew it would freak her if I stopped going to dancing. She'd paid for a whole term of ballet, tap, and modern and it cost a fortune. And it's funny, once I stopped going to classes, I found I hated dancing instead of loving it. And just thinking about it made me angry.'

'It's easy to do bad things when you're angry,' I say consolingly. 'She'll be thrilled that you are dancing Beauty, won't she? And you'll be able to show her the video that Ellen has made. There's probably five minutes of you and half an hour of Cara, but never mind.'

'Cara's got to be an awful little show-off,' Crystal says. 'Being in so many numbers and helping you with the babies has gone to her head.'

'Yes, she bosses Ellen around as if she's a slave. But she'll come down to earth with a bump when the show is over. We've all been there and done it, haven't we.' We share a smile.

'That boy Reece, the really good-looking one, whose party we're going to. Does he have a girlfriend?'

'Do you think he's good-looking?' I ask in surprise.

'Yeah, I said to you when we met him that I thought he was fit.'

'Oh, I thought you meant Joshua, the older brother. Now he is heart-throb material.'

'I didn't rate him,' she says dismissively. 'I thought he was up himself and a snob. He couldn't be bothered to talk to us, could he?'

'No . . . But I shouldn't hold out too much hope for Reece. He seems to be hopelessly gone on Ellen.'

'Ellen!' Crystal says with surprise.

'Yes, she's far too old for him. But there you are. "The course of true love never did run smooth." And she seems pretty keen on him too.'

'Oh.' Crystal looks disappointed. 'No chance there then.'

'Never mind,' I say smiling. 'You'll soon forget about him when you get to Disneyland. There'll be lots of gorgeous American boys with white teeth and suntans.'

'Suppose so,' she says forlornly. 'I just thought Reece was lovely. And what with him asking me along to his party like that—I thought maybe he liked me too.'

'Yes,' I say sympathetically. 'But I think he's just extra nice to anyone who is even remotely associated with Ellen. It doesn't mean anything else.'

I feel sorry for her. I have learnt through bitter experience that it is all too easy to build dreams out of nothing.

Later in the day when we arrive at the theatre I have stage fright. Or maybe it's life fright. I have been in shows since I was a toddler but I have never had a fit of the panics like this. My hands shake and I feel sick. Ellen makes me a cup of chamomile tea and gives me Rescue drops in water.

Everyone starts to arrive and Ellen helps me with the babies. Like Cara they are completely wiped out with excitement. I quieten them down with some of the songs we have learnt and by calming them I calm myself.

By the time the half hour is called by the stage manager I am beyond nerves. I slip down to the wings to check that the flower fairy wands are in place. One of my jobs is to hand them out as the little ones go on stage. The audience is coming into the theatre. I stand for a moment and listen to the familiar noise of the auditorium filling up. I always think it sounds like a great animal getting settled and comfortable.

The little ones from my baby group open the show. They are the bees in the flower fairy dance. I hear a collective murmur of pleasure and audible 'Ohs' from the audience. Their mothers will be collecting them at the interval and my life will get a little easier. Until then they are my responsibility. I cross my fingers and pray hard while they are on stage, ready in the wings to call out instructions or to creep on to rescue anyone if it is really necessary. I couldn't be more stressed if I had given birth to them all myself.

They are brilliant! No one falls over, or cries or wets their pants. They don't all manage to keep in time with the music, although they have been fine in rehearsal. But no one cares. It adds to their charm when they get things a bit wrong. Total love and pleasure is spilling out from the audience for them, because they are tiny little three year olds and they've learnt a dance and are doing it on a stage for the very first time. I am bursting with pride.

At the beginning of the second half Mrs Valente goes

on stage and speaks to the audience. 'I would like you to know that the finale of the show is slightly different to the version in your programme. Due to an injury, the part of the Beast in the final number will be danced by Rose Asquith and the part of Beauty will be danced by Crystal Asquith. Rose and Crystal have learnt these new roles in three days and have worked extremely hard to ensure that the show ran according to plan. I hope you will appreciate their hard work. I certainly do.'

There's lots of clapping from the audience and I find my cheeks growing hot because Ash is sitting out there somewhere in the auditorium. At least now he will know that I can do something right and I don't always make a hash of things.

It seems like only seconds later that the second half is drawing to a close and it is time for Crystal and me to perform. I can't believe it has gone by so quickly. Yet strangely, when Crystal and I take up our position, time seems to stop. Being on stage and waiting for the music seems like the longest moment of my life. I do deep breathing and try not to panic.

Then the curtain rises and the overture begins and I am suddenly lost in a different world. All around me is darkness and heat but my realm is the white coolness of the spotlight and my heartbeat is the rhythm of the music. It's almost a shock when we finish our dance and the last bar of music dies away. It's the thunder of the applause that brings me back to the here and now. I look at Crystal bemused. She is looking dazed. I take her hand and we walk to the front of the stage. There is a moment's pause while I take off my head-dress. Then Crystal curtsies and I bow (because I am a nominal boy). We have to take three curtain calls. The audience is shouting and clapping as if they've all won the lottery.

'I think the girl done good, hats off to Crystal,' I say to Ellen when we finally get back to the dressing room.

'I think the girls done good. You were both amazing.

I watched from the wings and I cried. When you were being beastly and hurt it was just too cruel. And I really believed that you loved each other at the end. It was so beautiful,' Ellen says with a sigh.

I give Ellen a hug and thank her. But all I can really think about is Ash. I wonder what he thought of it.

I hadn't realized how much I have been looking forward to seeing him. During the show I have been too busy to count the minutes. But inside my heart I have been waiting for him as a hibernating animal waits for spring.

I collect Crystal and Cara and we go front of house to meet Mum. She kisses us all and tells us how wonderful we were. Then she says, 'I thought I'd take you all to Nelson's for tea. A special treat because you have worked so hard on the show.'

And when I hear these words I feel almost ill with grief.

'Is that all right, Rose? Have you got a headache?' Mum asks. 'I thought it would be a lovely treat to go out for a meal. Did you have other plans?' she adds suddenly, looking stricken.

'Oh no! It will be lovely. I didn't have anything arranged,' I lie quickly. I can't remember the last time we went out for a meal or even a cup of tea. I can't possibly let Mum know that I had hoped to have pizza with Ellen, Ash, and the Brownes. 'Crystal and I are going to a party later on. I told you—do you remember—a birthday party at Monty's? But we'd love to go out for tea.'

'Yes. I thought it would be a treat for Cara, as she can't go to the party,' Mum says.

'Is Hamish coming?' I ask.

'I didn't ask him,' Mum says, looking embarrassed.

'Where is he? I rather thought he might come to see my show,' I say, rather hurt.

'I didn't ask him,' Mum says again.

'Why not?' I ask.

Mum says guardedly, 'I thought you might resent him coming along to your special day.'

'I don't know where you got that idea from,' I say huffily. 'I think he's an absolute hero, if you must know. And he's my friend as much as yours. I should have invited him myself. If I had some credit on my phone I'd ring him now. He likes Nelson's.'

'Does he?' Mum says, surprised.

'Yes he does,' I say firmly. 'Go and ring him,' I add, because, if I'm not going to be seeing Ash until later this evening, at least one of us will be happy in the meantime.

Mum says, 'I suddenly remembered during the show. I'm sure I still owe Mrs Valente some money for the costumes. Did I ever give you a cheque?'

'No, you didn't but it doesn't matter. You don't owe her any money. It's all taken care of. Hamish will explain. Go and ring him now,' I say.

I find Ellen and explain about Mum's plan. 'Just come and see Reece,' she says. 'He thought you were amazing and wants to congratulate you.' Ellen takes hold of my arm and walks me over towards the door. I see the Brownes and Ash before she does, she's so short-sighted. Josh is in shades, looking bored. Nothing new there then. But I hardly notice him. It's Jessica I can't take my eyes off. She is leaning up against Ash, her arm linked through his, and she is talking so urgently to him that her face is nudging his shoulder.

The sight of them together, so close, so friendly, so much a couple, snatches the breath from my lungs. I stop so abruptly that Ellen nearly falls over. I turn away fast, scared they might notice us. I begin to gabble to Ellen telling her I have to go straight back to the dressing-room, rabbiting about hair straighteners left on and the theatre being in imminent danger of burning down. I must get away. I must be alone and give my thudding heart and racing mind a chance to slow down.

I run back to the dressing-room. It is deserted; a pair of forgotten tights, a scrunchy, and discarded tissues litter the floor. Like a robot I pick them up; anything is better than facing up to the thoughts inside my head. But then, when the room is tidy, I have to think. I sit down at the mirror and look at my reflection. Then I hide my face in my hands.

The full implication of what I have seen in the foyer hits me. Ash and Jessica—a couple. Jessica is keen on Ash. I can see that now. It's a thought that has been festering in my mind since Jessica's horrible party. I'm sure one reason she invited me was as a lure to get him to go along. But what about Ash? Is it a case of 'the boy doth protest too much'? When he says that Jessica is the most stupid girl he knows does he really mean he fancies her?

Jessica and Ash—a couple—it will be hell on earth for me. They'll be dancing together and snogging at the party. And when we go back to school it will be the usual scene with Jessica and her boyfriends. In the cloakroom it'll be whisper, whisper, little titbits of gossip—just enough to keep everyone hanging on her every word. I shall have to endure Jessica laughing and coyly giving details about what he's said and what she replied and where they'd been and, worst of all, what they'd done. And this time it won't be some holiday romance boy, whose face we'll know from the photos, or some lad from the sixth form. This time it will be Ash she will be telling everyone about. How he kisses, what aftershave he wears, the crazy ways he loves her, and the secrets they share. Oh-my-goodness-this-is-mind-blowingly-terrible.

The very idea of it all drives me into a frenzy. A frenzy of grief and anger and jealousy. It just doesn't fit—it is all wrong—it is a miss-match. Ash and Jessica are not meant to be together. And how do I know that? It's quite simple. It is Ash and I who should be a couple. Why has it taken me so long to work it out? It seems so completely right and straightforward now I've thought about it. Me and Ash being together—not just as best friends—but as boyfriend and girlfriend—seems as natural as Monday following Sunday and night following day.

My face in the mirror is radiant with emotion. All I need to do is to see him and talk to him. Then reality kicks in. I can't very well walk up to him and say: 'Blow out sleek-haired, sophisticated, sexy Jessica and go out with little old me. I may have frizzy hair, no boobs, and a mouth like the channel tunnel, but you and me, boy, well, we are made for each other.'

I might have sat there all night, see-sawing between joy and misery. Joy that I am so completely in love with the best boy in the world and misery because I might have lost any chance of ever making him love me. But Crystal comes to get me.

'That boy is hanging around outside the theatre, everyone else has gone. I think he's waiting for you.'

'Boy?'

'The one from next door . . .'

I move so fast she has to run to keep up with me. Mum and Cara are waiting in the foyer.

'Are you ready to go, darling?' Mum asks anxiously.

'Yes, yes,' I say impatiently. Through the glass of the doors of the theatre I can see the outline of broad shoulders.

I race through the door into the rain. Ash is out there, looking at the photos of the show that are on display. His shoulders are hunched against the drizzle. He must have been waiting around for ages because his hair has dampened to the colour of autumn leaves and his face is wet with rain. He needs mopping with a tissue, or kissing, or both. I stop abruptly a good distance from him and try to look nonchalant.

'I thought I might have missed you,' he says.

'No . . . I'm here,' I say stupidly.

'Just wanted to tell you I thought your dance was ace. Really brilliant.'

'Thanks, thanks a lot.'

'It was great,' he says. 'Anyway. I'll see you later. You are coming to the party, aren't you?'

'Yes.'

'I'll see you then.'

'Yes, you'll see me then.'

He walks off as Mum and the others join me. I can't speak because I am so happy. He said he'd see me then. He wouldn't say that unless he really wanted to see me, would he?

Having tea at Nelson's is great. Hamish arrives and he and Mum discuss what work she can have done on the house now there is money coming in from the record deal. Mum agrees that they can look at the trees together—which must mean she really trusts him. Hamish laughs and shakes his head and says he'll not touch a twig unless she agrees to it. With every minute that ticks by I feel more excited because soon it will be time for the party and I will see Ash.

When we are home Cara goes to bed and Crystal and I get ready to go out.

'Do you ever look at your clothes and hate them all?' Crystal asks, when we are doing our make-up together in my room. 'Mum says we can go shopping in the States, which is just as well. I've put on loads of weight. I can hardly get my denim skirt done up.'

'You haven't put on weight, silly girl. You are just growing. That's what you are meant to do at your age.' I look at her critically. 'I might have just the thing for you.' I go to my wardrobe and take out my precious embroidered jeans. They have never looked so lovely. I don't know how I can bear to give them away.

I swallow hard. 'I bought these with all my birthday money last year and I liked them so much I hardly wore them—which was totally stupid because I grew out of them. They should just fit you. Would you like them? They're from Top Shop,' I add a bit defensively.

'Rosie! They're gorgeous. Really—can I wear them? They are heaps nicer than anything I've got.'

'You can have them to keep, if you'd like them. I told Ash I would take them to the Oxfam shop—but when it came to it I couldn't do it. I'm glad they are going to a good home.'

She gives me a hug, takes the jeans and pulls them on. They do look sensational on her.

'Have you got something nice to wear?' she asks.

'Yes, my black trousers and the T-shirt your dad sent,' I say bravely.

'Oh,' she says. I can see she thinks that it is really boring.

'Actually, I think I've got something even better,' I say suddenly. I start to root around in my drawer. Right at the bottom, neatly folded and brand new, is a T-shirt Ash gave me after a charity event. It has a cartoon dog on the front and the logo 'A dog is for life, not just for Christmas'. It's miles too big for me and hangs over the top of my trousers like a PE shirt. But I don't care. It's the message that matters.

'You're not going to wear that?' Crystal says aghast.

I don't reply. I just smile and nod.

Postscript

Monty's is packed. Most of Reece's year is here. They are all very noisy and excited, which I suppose is what we were like at their age. Ellen holds on to my arm and looks nervous. As if by magic Crystal gets talking to some boy and disappears into the crowd. She seems to have got over her disappointment over Reece.

'Can you see Reece anywhere?' Ellen asks me anxiously.

'No, but here comes Joshua, looking pleased with himself, as usual,' I say with a groan. I can't believe how much I have changed since the last party. I am not thrilled to see him. In fact the sight of him makes me feel embarrassed and stressed. I can't believe how much time I've wasted thinking about him.

'Hi there, sexy chick,' he says to me. He grins and slides his arm around my shoulders, and tries to pull me away from Ellen. 'Come and have a drink.' It isn't a question, it's a command. His tone and the casual way he touches me is totally irritating.

'No thanks,' I say abruptly. I pull away from his arm

and try to put some distance between us. This is difficult because the whole place is heaving.

He isn't the least put off by my lack of enthusiasm; in fact his hands slide around me. Oh-my-goodness-this-is-awful-he-is-all-over-me-like-a-rash!

'Have you seen Reece?' I ask, giving him an elbow in the ribs. He seems to take this as some kind of sexual overture because his grip on me tightens.

'The birthday boy is somewhere around,' Joshua says casually. His eyes aren't focused. I suddenly realize that he's already fairly sloshed.

'Come on, babe. I've been waiting for you. I've got a bottle of vodka hidden away. I'll share it with you.' He tweaks at my T-shirt and laughs.

'Don't do that!' I say. But he does it again and then slides his arms around me like some awful snake.

My temper flares. 'Look—piss off, will you!' I say—getting to work with both of my elbows to free myself. Then Ellen spots Reece and yanks me away.

I see Joshua's face, blank with surprise and annoyance, as we push through the crush of people and leave him alone.

'You really don't like him any more, do you, Rosie?' Ellen asks.

'Was it that obvious?'

'Yes, I thought you were going to slap him,' she says anxiously.

'He's lucky I didn't. But don't let it spoil your party. He'll get over it.'

'Reece says Joshua's really mean when he's angry,' Ellen says a bit fearfully.

'Oh, for heaven's sake, Ell! I'm not scared of Joshua Browne. He can't do anything to me!'

'He gets nasty when he drinks, Rose.'

'Ellen, I can take care of myself. Don't worry. Look—here's Reece.'

Reece hugs her as if they have been parted for years.

It's really sweet. 'Come on,' he says. 'The DJ is just about to start the music. But first I'm going to thank everyone for coming.'

He pulls Ellen with him up onto the edge of the stage where the speakers and deck are set out. There's a big cheer from all his friends when they see him. He stands with his arm around Ellen while he speaks into a mike. 'Thanks for turning up, folks. The bar is free. Food will be ready in an hour. Thanks for all the gifts you brought me. I just want you all to say "Hi" to my best birthday present of all—my girlfriend, Ellen.'

All the kids laugh and chorus 'Hi, Ellen'. Obviously Reece and Ellen's romance is popular among his friends.

'Stand still while I take a photo!' someone shouts. Ellen and Reece move closer into a proper hug and then start a long kiss. It all might have been fine—a lovely romantic start to Reece's birthday party. But there is a dark figure behind them, climbing on top of one of the big speakers and turning his back on the crowd.

Then, right above Reece and Ellen's heads appears a naked white bum. Joshua is mooning. The crowd collapses with helpless laughter. Everyone is creased. Apart from Reece and Ellen who are looking stunned. They can't see what is happening. I watch as Ellen's face crumples. It's horrible. I can't get to her to explain what is going on or protect her. She thinks the ghastly raucous laughter and wolf whistles are something to do with her and Reece and their shared kiss. She pulls away from Reece's arms and makes a run for it. I shove my way through the braying crowd and race after her.

Ash and I both get to her at the same time. 'I'm going to kick that bastard into next week,' Ash growls. 'He won't want to show off his backside when I've finished with him.'

'Ash—he's a total waste of space and he's not worth bothering with. And he's certainly not worth getting into trouble for. Let's get Ellen sorted out,' I say. 'Come on, Ash, quickly. She's getting totally hysterical.'

Ellen is weeping so much she can hardly stand. Ash and I half carry, half drag her outside and along the street.

'The Acropolis,' I say breathlessly.

It's the dingiest coffee bar in town and thankfully it is deserted. It also has booths so you can sit in relative privacy.

'Is she drunk?' the woman behind the counter says.

'No!' I snap furiously. 'Just upset.'

'I don't want any trouble.'

'There won't be any trouble. She'll be fine in a minute. Three coffees, please,' Ash says.

We get Ellen sat down and I give her a big hug. 'Listen, Ell, listen to me. They weren't laughing at you and Reece. Listen . . . it was Joshua.'

It takes ages to get her calmed down. And I can see by her face that she is starting with a migraine. 'Have you got your headache tablets with you? Take one now.'

'I'll go and wash my face,' Ellen says.

'Shall I come with you?' I ask anxiously.

'No. I'm fine. Thanks.' She manages a wobbly smile.

Ash and I are left alone, staring at each other over the narrow Formica table. I stir my cup of cold coffee.

'Snap,' I say, looking up at him with a little smile, because he is wearing his dog T-shirt that is the same as mine—only his is three sizes bigger and well worn.

'I've never seen you wear it before. I thought you didn't like it,' he says.

'I love it. I've been saving it for best,' I lie. 'We ought to try to get Ellen back to the party,' I add. 'Reece will be doing his nut wondering where she is.'

'I'll take you both back and then I'm off home,' Ash says moodily. 'I can't face looking at that chuffing moron Joshua. I might lose my rag completely and stick one on him.'

'Won't Jessica be upset if you leave?' I mutter. I sip my coffee even though it is scummy and disgusting.

'Jessica will have to find someone else to moan to. I've done my best so far this evening to be her counsellor. At the end of the day, no one can sort her problems out but her,' Ash says wearily.

'What's the matter?' I ask, sneaking a glance at him. He's not talking about Jessica as if they are a couple. If anything he sounds a bit cheesed-off and irritable.

'The Brownes have friends in America who they've been visiting and, while they were there, Jessica fell big time for the son. He's coming over here to study in the autumn and she's desperate to get together with him. From what she's told me, it's obvious that he's not interested in her. But Jessica thinks that if she gets thinner, blonder, and even more perfect then he'll eventually fall in love with her. She hasn't worked out that you don't love people because they are perfect.'

'Thank goodness for that!' I exclaim. 'Maybe there's still hope for me—even though I am a bloody lunatic.'

He reaches across the table and touches me. Our fingers tangle. Eventually he manages to get hold of my hand. He says, 'I'm sorry, Rosie. I was out of order to say that to you.'

'Oh no you weren't . . .' I say bravely. 'My head was full of bonkers ideas and I'm glad you told me the truth. That's what friends are for.'

'Yes.' He looks down at my T-shirt and smiles.

'Please come back to the party for a little while,' I whisper, because I will go crazy if I don't have a chance to get close to him.

'If your dog will dance with my dog I might,' he says.

'I think they are meant to be together,' I say carefully.

Then, as if on cue, we chorus together: 'A friend is for life not just for Christmas.' That makes us laugh. And I know then that everything is going to be perfect—or as nearly perfect as life can ever be in an imperfect world.

Other books by Julia Clarke:

You Lose Some,
You Win Some

ISBN 0 19 275327 4

Day One of Mum being away and the battle lines of our life have been drawn. No comfort—no crying—no kissing: because nothing is wrong—is it?

Cesca refuses to accept that Mum has gone. She's just helping out at the hotel, isn't she? Because of the foot-and-mouth outbreak? She'll be back soon and everything will get back to normal, won't it?

But then Cesca learns the secret that has split up her family and she has to believe that Mum has gone for good. How can she cope with everything that is going on—the aftermath of the foot-and-mouth epidemic and the loss of their animals; her on/off relationship with Jon—when Mum is not there to help her? And how will the rest of the family manage: Dad and Gerry and Ollie, who is just a baby? Trying to come to terms with all this, Cesca has to find a strength she didn't know she had . . .

Between You and Me

ISBN 0 19 275382 7

I'd always been lucky Jade. At home, Mum and Dad's perfect princess. At school, teacher's pet and joined-at-the-hip bestest friends with Jack.

Then, that fateful September, it all changed . . .

Sybil, looking as if she'd just climbed out of a rock star's bed, arrived at school. And Jack got the blues so bad it almost broke my heart. Then my art project sent me nosing around in unknown territories. I uncovered a past that included dark, moody Fin and endless secrets.

It was like a jigsaw. And now that the puzzle is solved, the final picture may not be perfect. But, between you and me, I wouldn't change a thing.

Summertime Blues

ISBN 0 19 275196 4

It's amazing how much I can glean from listening to one half of a telephone conversation. I hear whisper, whisper, and then, slowly, half sentences . . . Then the penny drops. The realization that my parents are fighting over me, and that neither of them wants me, hits me like a blow in the belly.

This is the start of a long, painful summer for Alex. He has no choice but to go to Yorkshire with his mother and her new partner, away from his friends, his home, and his A level studies. He just knows he is going to hate it all, the isolation and quiet of the countryside, the cold, primitive cottage, and most of all, Seth. His one thought is to get away, back to civilization in London. But then he meets Louie, who looks after abandoned and ill-treated animals, and Faye, Seth's daughter, and suddenly the summer is full of new experiences and challenges which will change Alex's life for ever.

'Clarke sharply conveys the sadness and frustration of an only child who doubts if his existence is worthwhile.'

The Times

'A readable and revealing account of growing up.'

Kids Out

'written with such pace, humour and believable, adolescent angst that I found it both moving and compelling.' *Books for Keeps*